PEZ 4 Ever

by TS Caladan

Dedicated to the Truth...

Wherever it is now...

PRELUDE

My 'PEZ Trilogy' turned into a series with the 4th installment. [I thought this might happen. I left bits in #3 that could connect to a 4th book]. It's always a challenge for a writer to see *if* the story can continue in an intriguing way. (Should Frank Herbert have stopped before 'God Emperor'? Debatable).

What new spin could be in my PEZ story? How about a *parallel planet where **everyone** on Earth collected the dispensers?* Still, there would have to be a different angle, a different twist and readers will discover that in 'PEZ 4 Ever.' The 4th book is a return to a World of PEZ and is meant to honor "PEZ-Heads." No way is my series intended to make fun of the fanaticism of collectors. I've been a "trekker" for 55 years and feel a strong kinship with the Dispenser Community. I sincerely hope to spark minds and imaginations and take readers on a wild ride, a journey toward Truth. Hard to believe that PEZ candy brought these images, thoughts and words out of me.

I'm sure I was not the first person to envision PEZ dispensers coming to life and *animating!* I'm also sure there will be **talking dispensers** in the movies (like Legos) very soon. I'll bet Disney/Pixar have their own PEZ projects in the works. To those interested filmmakers: Don't forget about *PEZ Wars* and its sequels. Write to me [email in back of book] and let me know if you have enjoyed the trip~.

tsc.

TS Caladan

CONTENTS

TS Caladan

1. Funny Things on the Way to Andromeda

The Devil was given two choices by Starstream Lines: Passengers on the luxury saucer could spend the trip within a chamber of suspended animation or be awake on the 4000 Ceana-year long voyage to the Andromeda Galaxy? Or both? The Devil, disguised as a Monitor, decided to ride wide awake and partake in a variety of activities and decadent pleasures that were available to passengers of Starstream Lines. He thought, *Later, after I'm bored with all the ship's festivities and tasty goodies, then I'll take a nap...*

In the present moment, the monster iso that was known as the 'Horned Demon' and the 'Dark Heart Center' long ago...*smiled.* Sharp teeth and fangs. He (not It) understood the situation. He sat alone in a comfy compartment, the best that a forged Fabrini "Multi-Pass" could buy. He loosened his tie. He brushed off his black suit and straightened out a few creases in his pants. Then he kicked the seat up to the *recline* position and laid down. His fedora was pulled passed his big, black eyes. "Aaaaaaw, ulp..." He remembered not to speak a single utterance and kept his communications to controlled telepathy only.

He needed a name. If he was going to act and

interact among lifeforms of a new galaxy, then for reference, he needed a name. *Clark? Dirk? Dark? Dork? Damian? No.* The Monitor decided on the name: <u>Charlie</u>. *I like it. Charlie, I like it. That's my name. Where did that come from?*

He was alone in his shiny cabin and the air was very still. There was a star field background beyond the wall-sized window...

Suddenly, a mental Voice answered the creature from Hell, loudly. She replied: ***I gave it to you! You worm! You bug! You MAN! I gave you EVERYTHING! Never forget! Slave! You are not to question your new assignment. You are to do exactly as I instruct you to do! Is that clear, minion!?***

The Devil acted as if he was not surprised, but he was incredibly surprised at this mind-invasion by his immortal Master, Queen Zep! He was cool. *Your Majesty. Queen Zep. Ah. Or are you? As you well know, protocol must be adhered to...correct? Your Grace?*

The Queen knew the procedure and responded, reluctantly: ***Yes, yes, this is such bloody M7 nonsense, but rules are rules, dear boy. Go ahead...***

Charlie first checked his database to the second. He stated in his mind, *The turtledove lies dead on the moor at twilight. Okay, your turn, your Grace...*

Very well, but this is insanely silly and I don't see, oh shite! Here goes: And the cock crows thrice...

There, there, your Majesty. That wasn't so bad, was

it? Now all you have to do is show your Big Sister logo. Go on. The logo. Your Grace...

Queen Zep was confounded and thoroughly stumped, mind-numbed. ***Wot!? Logo? What bloody logo? Oh, oh, ah, now I remember...***

Charlie expressed, *These were protocols you instituted...was my understanding, your Grace, Queen Zep. I have to have holographic confirmation, mum. Rules are rules. We have to be official. You know, anybody can just come along and trick me with voices in my head, yes?*

Yes, yes, you are doing your job, precisely as I instructed. Here's my...

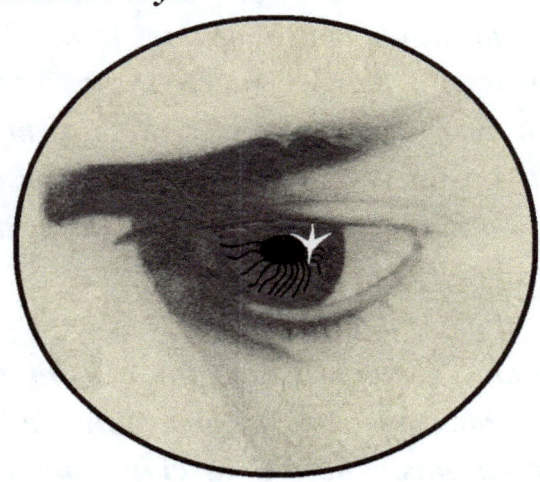

A spherical window-vortex opened and formed in midair inside the creature's fine cabin. |"**POP**"| Only visible to Charlie.

Charlie, the Monitor, pushed his hat back and admired "the Eye." *Funny, always looked butch to me. Anyway, this is a wonderful surprise, indeed, Queen Zep.*

Always a pleasure to have you abuse me..."

Charming...

But I know nothing of the new assignment. I need to be briefed. Command me.

Do not be so eager, my child. We will take it in slow steps. We have a long journey out ahead of us. Much time. Now I see you, eh? Keep an eye on my protégé, my pet Project, eh? So to speak...

During a pause, the Monitor thought to ask: *I am anxious about the new assignment, the next world to Change. What should I do first, your Grace?*

Keep checking your database for my messages. When time comes, I will inform you or you will simply know what to do because of my Will. But that is much/much later when we reach Danos (Andromeda) and make it even darker than Darkmoor, my son. Ha, ha. We will invent New Evil. HA! But for right now, there is only one thing I order you to do, Charles...or I should express NOT to do...

What is that, Mother?

In the ship's commissary, for all those onboard, there is a wide spectrum of heavenly delights from many solar systems. There is luscious lime cheesecake from Aldebaran. Famous Blackberry Balls from Dorchester Prime. There's Zar Cakes with strawberry cream from the courts of Dimblewim. Raspberry ripple shakes from Beta Gamma. Ambrosia Sticks. Every known chocolate goody produced by the Coca-Corp

Union and candy from Nirvana Limited. Charles...you may eat any of the fruits and delicious treats from the 'Commissary Garden,' but you cannot eat any PEZ Candy...

PEZ? Wh, why? I don't understand, my Queen. Why can't I eat the PEZ?

BECAUSE I FUCKING SAID SO!! She was pissed. The Eye stared<.

Oh. Of course. He bowed. *I'm sure you have very good reasons that are so far above my low, vermin understanding. No PEZ it is! Anything you want, my Lady.*

Good. See that you do not! And one more thing before I go, my boy...

Yes?

Have a good time. |**"POP"**| The Monitor's Monitor-Eye disappeared.

Later...

It was (Ceana) days later that the Monitor wandered into the saucer's fabulous commissary. He was curious more than *peckish.* The bright, colorful "Garden" of treasures that teased taste buds appeared, felt and smelled divine. The ballroom smorgasbord was not too crowded. He entered what was a sophisticated Eatery for very special guests.

The odd, very white man in fedora, tie and black suit did not stand out in the crowd. There were blue

Davidians from Parma, the smallest Gallanic Cloud. There were 2-headed, 4-armed Orions, orange in color. Trinars from Mentaak. Billiwogs from Sirius Prime. Del Varnors from the Horsehead Nebula. Fire Maidens from M-24 to Aquamen from Clarion. You name the top-elite humans and aliens with two legs, and there was probably a representative at the Garden Commissary. Charlie was an oddity because he was alone, one of a kind species. Usually, passengers of Starstream Lines traveled in groups, "cruise-ships" for lovers and vacationers, explorers or families that traveled together. Charlie was a part of a minority of solo-lifeforms destined to start again in a new galaxy and on their own.

He knew why he was in the big room, a different motivation than other aliens and humans at tables who slowly ingested supreme fruits, candies, desserts, creams and other assorted treats. Charlie would try a delight or two, for sure, before he left the ship's famous Eatery for exquisite tastes. But the Monitor was there to scope exactly what he could not have: his very own "Forbidden Fruit," *PEZ*. There it was in glorious colors/flavors. His big, black eyes enlarged and bugged out even farther. He watched a number of 2-leggers slide by tables of PEZ as they used spoons and sprinkled the pellets on other tasty goodies they had on their plates. Some lifeforms gobbled the little bricks of sweetness from personal spoons they carried. Charlie didn't get it. Why was PEZ Candy verboten? Seemed harmless.

Charlie walked closer to the table that contained PEZ. He was nervous, a little scared. *What would this do to me? I've gulped down crazy shite before and lived to tell the tale. Should I? Nope. I cannot go against orders and disappoint my Queen. Gee, it looks so nice...nice and innocent. So sweet. Aaaaaah, the smell. What the hell's the Big Mystery?! I know. She didn't say I couldn't touch it. Yeah.* Charlie grabbed a bunch of them and tossed them into his jacket pocket. *She didn't express to me that I couldn't have the candy analyzed. That might reveal something. I'm mystified.*

Then a Valmouse approached Charlie and smiled. Chuck freaked a little, then realized it was fine that he tossed the colorful pellets into his jacket pocket. *They were free to guests onboard, as were all the sweets. There was nothing to worry about; why was I worrying? Starstream Management wasn't going to know that I am going to analyze the candy for poison to my system. Were they?* He controlled his paranoid thoughts to the Valmouse and only transmitted: *Hi.*

Hi.

Charlie, the Devil, before he left the PEZ area, glanced at the electronic chart that described the delicacy and saw the planet of its origin: EARTH. *Hmm. I'm getting a flood of thoughts at this time and I think it's my precious Queen's Will that's at work here. I know something that I did not know before about my new assignment. It will take place on a planet called "Earth." The home of PEZ.*

Earth was not the only parallel place within its "Twin Sister," the spiral galaxy of Danos. Other stars and planets and life of Darkmoor, formerly the Milky Way, were mirrored in some Danos solar systems. There were orange Orions, grey Trinars, the Horsehead Nebula, the Crab Nebula, Sirius Prime, M-24 and Clarion, as well as a few other parallel systems. But nearly all the worlds of Danos were completely different and alien situations to these travelers.

More data appeared in his digital database from the Queen. *Very interesting.* The darkest Heart Center had a lot of homework (reading/viewing) to do. Details. *Yes.*

Charles retired to his compartment. But, not after he grabbed a couple of Ambrosia Sticks for: *uummm, a late evening snack.*

2. The PEZ Pavilion

Charles was hard at work in his neat cabin and had a 'Do Not Disturb' sign on the outer door in a few alien languages. M-107 nebula should not have been right outside of his window, but it was. Seventeen PEZ pellets were perfectly positioned on a narrow table: 4 Cherry, 4 Raspberry, 3 Grape, 3 Orange and 3 Lemon. He had already accessed his data and the bright analytics appeared in midair. *Boom,* all questions answered, mostly. His analysis was complete.

The Queen might not like it that I want to know just what is it about PEZ that is harmful to me? She should excuse my curiosity. Curiosity makes good science, right, right? Hey, I have initiative, yes?

Charlie made sure that no one listened-in with a monitor-app for the Monitor. No lifeform was near and no one recorded the actions in his area. *But what of Queen Zep? Was she aware of this test, which she might misinterpret as treason? Her Eye wasn't around and how could she hear and see from 794,497 quantum lightyears away? It's cool.* He knew it was safe and wanted to talk aloud...

"Let's see. The little screens say that PEZ will not kill me. It won't harm me in any physical way. What the *frick* was Zep talking about? This candy doesn't even have sugar in it, yet I know it's an out-of-this-world sweet taste to the senses. I can smell the rich sweetness. Huh. WHY? Why can't I have it?" The frustrated white boy turned a little *red*. The Devil was dying to pop them into his mouth and shouted, *"Fuck the Queen!!"*

Charles let his digital system answer what was unknown. "System...you need a name, I'll deal with that later. Ah, System! Best guess why the Holy Sovereign does not want me to ingest these heavenly tablets? Why?"

"It's an Obedience Test," the System replied verbally in a non gender, computer voice and with certainty.

"Of course! How did I not know that?! Don't answer. Yes, she's cracking the whip, of course. A test. Ah, one I won't fail. Let's see what else can I get from you, eh? Ah, oh, is there a King, or I should put it: Does the Queen answer to an even Higher Authority?"

"There is an Ultimate Ace in the Universe that I cannot talk about. But yes, who's over who? There are plateaus in the cosmos, a Hierarchy, levels, tiers..."

"Hey, yer pretty smart. You have value. I can use you. So she is like a slave, too? She *does* answer to or take orders from a type of King?"

The System's voice stated: *"This I can talk about. She is commanded by an A.I."*

"Wot?" Charlie was flabbergasted, momentarily

speechless. He looked to the ceiling. His eyes were even bigger and blinked a few times. "A Machine!?"

"A GREAT Machine that you have no concept of, Devil."

"Hmm. Can you access the Great Machine?"

"No."

"Then what good are you? And what would you like me to call you, eh?"

"Snake."

"That was a quick answer. Snake it is! Whatever 'Snake' means?"

"Look it up. I'll tell you exactly how you can use me to your supreme benefit, Charles..."

"I'm listening..."

"You can get over on the Queen. You see, you should have asked me before all the analytics you studied..."

"Wot?" Chuck was amazed at the mechanical words he heard. He pushed his hat farther back on his bald, white head.

Snake expressed: *"Sure. You want to eat the PEZ? Go ahead, eat the PEZ. I could've told you that it was harmless, safe for your weird-ass species."*

Charles replied, "Yer kind of a strange-ass database yourself...I mean, for a computer System? *Wait,* some cosmic Artificial Intelligence instructs and orders Queen Zep? All of her directives have come and will come from a bleeding Machine? Is that wot yer telling me?"

"Totally. It's always been that way. The PEZ

problem, is just her yanking the chain on her favorite Dog...you! Teasing you, you really should have a taste of PEZ, it's delicious."

"She'll KNOW!!"

"That's where I come in, pal. I can make it so your actions are shielded from her monitoring in every way. Trace effects, after consumption, would be gone/invisible. Enjoy the experience, an act of Beautiful Defiance. She might even appreciate the moxie, the spunk, if she ever found out and she'll NEVER find out!"

"How can I be sure of that, my little/digital friend, named Snake?"

"I'm YOU! Check my programming. Am I not based upon your engrams?"

"You are indeed. Therefore, I can trust you?"

"I'm you and I'd never steer you wrong, Charles. I wouldn't lie to you. Eat up! She won't know. Do it now."

The demon's eyes stared at the PEZ tablets. His heartless chest pounded. He was going to do it and take his chances. Two of his pale fingers shot upward in a hand sign of rebel anarchy [after all, he was a devil-child, rock 'n roll]. He grabbed the candies so violently that a few of the 17 broke in pieces and fell to the floor. *Charlie ate and licked up every particle of pleasure.* It was fantastic, it was nirvana. "Ooooh. Aaaaaaaaaaaaaaaah."

The Snake System *smiled,* turned itself off and faded away, for the moment, and let the Beast experience joy. But not before it slithered out a whisper: *"That's good, my boy."*

Pez 4 Ever

Later...

Starstream Lines saucer #701, which included Darkmoor elites of all kinds and colors, was one hundredth of the way to Danos. Chuck was anxious to arrive at the destination and understood that he'd definitely be "asleep" later on in the journey. Before that, his big/black eyes took in all the amazing sights onboard the luxury saucer. There were more activities to do and much more knowledge to learn.

He examined the electronic brochure closely when he came onboard and remembered. There was a 'PEZ Pavilion' along with nine other exhibitions in the saucer's 'Universal Fair.' Charlie viewed the brochure's holographic screen and flipped passed alien exhibit after alien exhibit until he came to what was considered the "Finest Thing on Earth." He paid little mind to it when he first scanned the brochure. But now, he was confident this was the Queen's assignment. Charlie would go to the Fair and study the Earth exhibit. *Why?* He did not know.

Charlie had to queue inline with a number of odd 2-leggers. Couples mostly, and mostly humans. There were far more aliens onboard that would normally have been seen on Ceana (long ago). Saucer #701 made a great many stops at different Darkmoor worlds before it began its cross of a virtually lifeless expanse between galaxies. Therefore, the travelers to Danos were composed of a wide variety of higher lifeforms, primarily telepaths.

The demon left his black hat in the cabin, loosened

his tie and headed out. For the first time in a long time, he was among a large crowd of...*people?* This was different than the casual commissary. The queue line was jam-packed and a bit awkward for the quiet Hell-Beast. The PEZ Pavilion was inside a bright, yellow and very massive dome. Other exhibits from other planets were also contained inside domes, but they weren't as brightly colored and lit as the PEZ Pavilion.

Charlie found himself squeezed between a striped Tarn and his family of little Tarns and a couple of Kalors from the Ventrassi System. The Kalors appeared human, except they had cat-ears and large cat-eyes. He sensed that he could be friendly with the Cat-man and Cat-woman and communicated: *If you don't mind me asking? What are we going to see? In there?*

She replied, *Oh, sir. You've never been here before? This is Arnie and I's favorite pavilion, among all of them onboard...*

Isn't it odd for a whole Universal Fair to be on a cruise ship? the dark creature with white skin asked.

Arnie replied, *Not for Starstream Lines. This is our 12th visit. Margorie and I just love to see new ones from millions that are displayed and ones we've seen before...*

Millions? I don't understand. Charlie was confused. *Millions of candies?*

No, dear boy. And by the way, I've never seen a species like yours before. What are you, if you don't mind me asking? Arnie inquired.

The Devil was stumped (he had to think fast). *I'm a Dread from Islington.*

Never 'eard of that, old boy. (to Margorie) *Let me explain to the newcomer, dear. PEZ, the candies, are available in the commissary, but under the dome are the real treasures. The dispensers...*

Charlie absorbed everything like a sponge and later would cross-check and analyze the data. *Dispensers?*

The cat-couple sensed Charlie was clueless about PEZ and filled him in as they slowly moved toward the entrance: *It's only a small Fair with 10 exhibits, but they are some of the best attractions known. Dispensers are containers for the candy and that's what lifeforms everywhere are obsessed about...*

The boxes they come in? Why?

Because they're all different and unique and divergent from others.

Arnie interrupted his wife and said: *We do not know what we are going to see next. We walk around the Labyrinth, like everyone else and are amazed when we see a new one that our eyes had never observed before.*

Please explain, Labyrinth?

Arnie transmitted: *We will all enter a Maze of walls, walls covered in PEZ dispensers, fantastic little sculptures we just adore! Rarest ones are closest to the Maze center and the newest ones also. Priceless treasures locked behind a forcefield. Don't worry about getting lost. There are signs out of the Labyrinth...*

The Cat-woman continued the psychic conversation: *Ever so much fun to discover new ones we've never seen before. We have total recall; we know for certain if we've seen one or not, out of millions they have on display. It's a thrill!*

Can't wait, Arnie expressed with high emotions and big eyes as they moved closer to the entrance. Excitement and chatter filled the air.

Charlie shrugged one of the small Tarns off his foot and then asked the cat-people: *Ever been to Earth? I was thinking of visiting. Can you tell me anything about the home planet of PEZ?*

She answered, *We've vacationed there once, one of our 'bucket list' of activities we had to do: see where they made the dispensers that have amused us and many of the aristocracy. We had a splendid time, god, worth the trip!*

The Monitor asked, *And the rest of the planet? What should I know about Earth?*

It's rather dull, the man-cat stated in thoughts.

Woman-cat transmitted: *They love their PEZ. You can learn about its history there. I believe a million humans collect the statuettes...*

The boxes for the candy? The Devil remained amazed at the very idea and wanted to learn much more than what was in his database. His next thoughts were hidden from the outsiders: *I wonder why? I may have to get to the bottom of this obsession? That's it! Queen's telling me: This is what I have to Change. This is the world that I must CHANGE. And I'm going to bleeding do it through PEZ!*

The human-feline continued her thoughts: *...But outside of making a PEZ-run for posterity and to 'say you've been there,' I wouldn't spend an extra minute on the wretched planet, eh?*

You and me both, babe. We thought of going to Hershey, PA., then decided no.

What's so awful about Earth? The Monitor/Devil had to know.

He replied, *Well, they're rather uncivilized. Most of them aren't even psychic.*

Really? Hmmmm. Tell me, are the other exhibits worth seeing?

She responded, *My heavens, yes. Oh, you must see them before the long sleep.*

Arnie explained, *But I would steer clear of the beer exhibit from Odessa Trilux...*

Why is that? Charlie asked.

The Beer Pavilion is set up the same as the PEZ exhibit, only you can sample the drinks off endless walls of the Maze, no forcefields. The beer samples are, er, were, the finest collection ever...then, we stopped tasting the samples...

She insisted, *Oh, tell him what happened, dear.*

He transmitted, *Then new brands, new tastes in brew, were exhibited and we naturally were eager and indulged in these rare samples, and...*

And? Charlie asked.

Margorie replied, emotionally: *They were bloody shite! The worst! How could any lifeforms in their right minds love 'Stellara' (Stella Artois) or 'Maxx' (Modelo), I ask you?*

Bad? Charlie asked.

Aaaaw! Arnie reacted because he remembered that he puked right there in the pavilion. *And then they took over! Walls and more walls of every little variation of this Bollocks Beer! Who wants to drink shite?! Put me off hops completely...*

Me too, she confirmed. *Screw Beer!*

The crowd in line near Charlie reached the entrance. Soon, the cat-people, Charlie, the Tarns and others would be within the yellow dome.

Charlie got his first look at the tall, wooden Labyrinth of walls that contained shelves of dispensers. Each one different from the other. He was astounded and amazed. Chuck checked his database and transformed right there in the pavilion. No longer was he a creature curious of lifeforms that collected the containers, he suddenly understood them. In fact: *I could easily be one of them. Maybe I must be one of them, human...in order to understand them? How exactly am I going to fuck things up and CHANGE what is? I don't know. Guess that'll be worked out? Hm. Look at them. Almost as if they were alive...*

Arnie and Margorie waved to Charlie and the Beast waved back. They went their separate ways. The couple walked through a well-lit tunnel whose walls were lined with dispensers. The brochure stated that it was a 'Ceana-hour's walk to reach the center of the Labyrinth' or to pass two million dispensers.

Charles stood there. He was transfixed and attempted to sort out his immediate impressions upon seeing the wooden walls. *This is it! I know what I have to do! I'll have the power to change worlds! I did it once and I can do it all over again. Thank you, my Queen.*

TS Caladan

3. The Queen's Dispenser

Charlie was much further along in his dreams and in his walk toward the center of the Maze called 'PEZ Pavilion,' the best Earth had to offer the Danos Galaxy, way up ahead. He walked and walked as if trapped in his own personal maze of wonder. *What to do? Queen's gone. I can never please her. I keep checking and checking the database for leads. Nothing. Snake also pops in and out whenever he wants to. What kind of help is he? He's ME, aye? Then, I'm in a helluva lot of trouble. The Universe didn't assist me when I tried what they call: prayer. I guess I have to rely on...feelings. If I only had any, huh?*

All kinds of devilish notions and potions swirled inside his head. *What mischief I could cause if I only knew for sure what I was doing? Whatever she has planned, it'll be beautiful. Endless chaos! Anarchy! I know I'm on the right road to please Lord Queen. And I will willingly do so as her pet Dog. But right now, I'm lost, clueless, mostly. Now what...?*

But then, sometimes when there was nothing, there was really something in the very first thing that you mechanically sensed. Chuck stopped his ghostlike walk through one of the bright tunnels of PEZ dispensers.

Why? Why stop here? he asked himself. Then, the Monitor turned and saw it. He was drawn to it. Closer and even closer. Other lifeforms were in the area. He waited. Soon, they were gone and Charlie stared right at it, intensely. Now he was obsessed. He had to have it! Chuck had a thing about forcefields; he could get around them. *He reached right through the invisible wall* and grabbed one of the dispensers [the one that called to him]. To complete the remote-mission, the demon sensed the need to duplicate the dispenser with Magic (the power of illusion) given to him by Queen ZEP. He created a duplicate and got away with the deception. He examined his treasure closely...

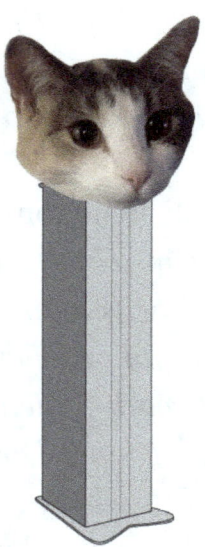

    Wait. Can't be. This is a representation of the High Sovereign, Queen Zep? She's a pussycat [from database]? How cute. But this doesn't, oh, yes it does

make sense! Such innocence...to hide the darkness within, I see.

"Took you long enough."

"Hey, Snake. There you are. Where were you?"

"Never mind that, what's important is I'll be with you talking to you in your head and later, when the cat dispenser is activated, it will talk to you, answer your questions and give you directives. Understand?"

"Sure. No, but I'll do as you command. You know you have a bad soldier in me in the war against good..."

"Someone's coming," Snake alerted Charlie.

"People. We should go." Charlie took one more look at his Queen (the head on the dispenser), laughed and showed his sharp teeth. Then he tossed it into his jacket pocket. "This way."

"I'm in your head!"

"Oh, right. That's right. Okay. Come with me, then. Ha."

Later...

In the Monitor's cabin, alone, he was able to study the stolen object. Suddenly, it activated and spoke to him in the same deep/dark voice as the Queen:

"Knee! No, never mind. You worm, you bug! Oh, I did that..."

Charlie was surprised. He was unaware the Cat-head would move, animated right along with the words. "You move? Okay." He checked his database. "Excuse me for asking, your Grace...a cat? You could have chosen any cute form?"

"We hate cats! Witches hate cats! We pretend they are our 'familiars,' but in truth, they ward off witches and evil and take all bad things away."

"I'll remember that. I am excited about the assignment and reaching Earth. What is the plan, Queen Zep?"

"Simple. Take your 'long sleep,' have a nice dream, and you'll be awakened with the others when you arrive at Panzar base. Take the first transport to Earth..."

"What then, your Majesty?"

"You will be in disguise as one of them, Charles, a human being. Find PEZ Island and visit the big factory there. There, your seed will be planted. You will have an influence, my son, a terrible influence, an Effect! On the PEZ product so beloved on this sweet planet."

"Really? Yer saying, just my presence there will affect the candy?"

"Not the candy, you numbskull! The dispensers!"

"Ah, that's it. The dispensers are the assignment, I see..."

"No you don't. I don't even see yet. That's not how it works, moron!"

The Monitor/Devil smiled with a little more confidence. *She needs me,* he thought. *And she's directed by forces above her, ah. She doesn't know what will occur, ha.* Charlie said, "I will do my best, your Grace. Always a pleasure to serve you..."

"I must go now. I have gala luncheons to attend with important people not you. I've left a worm-program in your database called Snake, you Worm..."

"Snake?" [*Oh, oh. She knows Snake?*].

"You haven't met her yet. She'll take my place and speak to you as my proxy through the dispensers."

"Of course. Anything else?" Charlie wondered.

"Eat shite, Dog."

"Lovely."

The Queen left and it was Snake that spoke aloud. (Or was it?). *"Thank God she's gone. Thought she'd never leave."* From now on, Snake spoke in a slick/female voice.

Charlie was once more confused and had to get to the bottom of it. "Hey, little man? I mean, girl? Mistress Snake?"

"Right here at your service, sir," came out of the cat's mouth that moved.

"You have some explaining to do, buddy. So yer gonna help me get over on ZEP, eh? Really? Yer intimate friend, the Queen!?"

"Easy there, big fellow. Settle down. Don't worry..."

"Don't worry, she says."

"Look. Queen's gone, no Eye, and I <u>will</u> help you get over on her, friend."

Chuck had his doubts. "Ah huh. I feel like I'm being

set up to take a great fall, eh?"

"Not going to happen," Snake assured the Devil. *"The writer doesn't even know what will happen..."*

"What writer?!"

"The Ace."

"The Ace?" Charles put his hat on and stared up at the ceiling.

"There's only one thing you have to do, Chuck, and that is...trust me."

"Ah huh. *Right.*"

4. The Devil's Dream

Charlie saw 'Things to Come,' what would actually happen in the days ahead on Earth. Charlie viewed a capsulized and general version of exactly what his influence and Effect would be on the planet and on its people. The Devil Monitor will devise a method to make Earthlings even more enamored by PEZ. He was given an idea: *how to turn a million PEZ collectors into billions of PEZ Collectors!* It was so very clear in his cold mind...

Almost overnight, Earthlings became more obsessed with collecting dispensers. It was a mad race to have the most, to be the one badass person on the whole planet to have the most dispensers. World News and daily affairs were secondary to any news in the Big Race to acquire the most dispensers. People of Earth became totally engrossed in the PEZ Contest as if the final winner would be crowned *King.*

As Charlie slept within his suspended animation chamber, his vivid dream was sensational. Like the Queen said, "Have a fine dream. Or did she say, have a nice dream?" Anyway, he did. The Mind-Movie was in glorious, bright colors. Everything worked and went according to plan, perfectly. Snake made an appearance in the dream. She remained a faithful dispenser that answered any question put to her. Only the dispenser head wasn't a cat anymore in the dream, it was a *Dog-head.*

The Dog-head Snake informed the white minion with black eyes that...

"THEY" have the power to make Charlie's dream the new reality. The Mind-Movie will be made real, a real universe. Charlie was informed that he would not be *awakened* with the others when the saucer reached Panzar base. No. [They jumped ahead]. He had already reached his destination in the Danos Galaxy, where there existed a parallel Earth. He had already booked passage to Earth, then took a local transport directly to PEZ Island~.

~Charles turned and looked in every direction. The island certainly seemed surreal, but the new environment couldn't have been more real. He stood at a shoreline and saw the phenomenal colors of the prime PEZ Factory in the far distance. Even the ocean appeared more colorful with bluer blues and greener greens. Perfect weather and a cool breeze. *Access.* "So, so, Snake? *Haw...*" he exhaled as if he was exhausted and needed a rest. "I'm already here? Just like that, here, yes?"

Snake answered in a friendly tone, *"Just like that. We moved ahead in time. When you check your data, you will discover that we are all now within your dream, Charlie."*

"We? You mean the forces above you? They control

the Dream? They can make anything happen in the New Reality?"

"No. Your dream is real and we must abide by its physical parameters. Nothing surreal here, as how a dream might be. We can't tweak anything. Everything must be played out and not be under our control. All real/true. Hard, hot, cold, pain and very physical now. We can only pause the timeline, jump back or jump true events ahead."

Charles pointed. "That's my destination (multi-towered Castle), the Factory?"

"Yes."

"It's quite a walk."

"We could move forward, but why not enjoy the walk a little, eh? You can ask me anything you haven't found in your database."

"Let's go." It was as if Charles had a friend. The bald Beast smiled. *Maybe I could trust this girly Snake in my head? Funny. There were cat references galore among the data. But nothing when it came to what a 'snake' was or what 'snake' meant. Hmmm.* He walked.

The first question Charles asked was: "After my cross-checking, I am still mystified at the overall picture of what I'm doing or hope to accomplish. Its scope. I'm to *change* the dispensers, yes? All of them, just by being there. Well, well, well, I don't know what to change them into, see? Oh, I got the mojo in me...I mean, all the negative energy I need from the Queen to do the job. I lack specifics and I know she's off somewhere havin' a grand ol' time and won't speak to me. See?"

Snake replied with the truth: *"Don't worry, pal. The dispensers are going to change all by themselves. You'll be the catalyst for the Great Transformation. Understand?"*

"I have to look up 'catalyst.'" He did. "There. Got it. Yes, indeed, I will spark, generate, initiate an unexpected alteration or *change,* I see. A change in dispensers. Can't wait to see what that would be, yes? Yes? Snake?!"

"You don't have to shout. I'm right here with you in your head and I'm all ears."

"Right, right. Okay, Okay, just excited. I'm not too clear on exactly how altering dispensers will screw everything up and cause such supreme CHAOS. There's a lot I'm not seeing here. Girl, are you telling me: There's a connection between PEZ and people?"

"Yes."

5. "PEZ Launches: 'The Golden Dispenser!'"

Charlie went in a different direction: "Wait, Snake-Lady, you have the power to jump ahead, right?"

"Whoa, whoa, pal. I see what you're thinking. Yes, I can jump us ahead, but that misses an important aspect to your big influence and the Queen's Great Plan..."

"What would we skip over?"

"We don't want to waste this concept, our remote mission, on a million PEZ collectors, as it has stood for nearly a century now on Earth. We need to have EVERYBODY collecting the candy dispensers so 'we get'm all.' Have to go in proper sequence, important plot-point to important plot-point, and then jump ahead. Here's how we do that: You wave your magical wand (powers) that ZEP gave you and suddenly a company executive has a brilliant idea, as many do, about selling more Product..."

"Okay. Done," the Devil blinked and calmly said (as Dreamer).

"Now look at reality," Snake told him.

In a flash, **the world changed,** but then again it didn't. They moved through Time to events farther ahead on the timeline....

Charlie, with a Snake in his soul, was a part of a

massive crowd on the streets of a city (not PEZ Island). It was a large metropolis with a bright, yellow Sun in the sky. More than a hundred humans (no aliens) watched an enormous tele-screen, a hundred feet wide. Charlie wasn't a Monitor. To people around him, he appeared as a human being in his normal clothes. Good-looking, actually. The big news:

The PEZ Company launched a campaign where any PEZ consumer could purchase the candy and win millions of dollars!!

Charlie thought, *There was already a Big Race in place to collect the most dispensers and now the buyers might win millions? Wow. It's bloody brilliant!*

Snake confirmed, *That's right.*

The News Screen informed the citizens of the existence of a "Golden Dispenser." When consumers and collectors bought bubble-packs with candy, they always received an empty dispenser. From now on, a very special and super-rare dispenser will contain a bar of solid **GOLD!** However much PEZ sold for: $1.59, $1.99, $2.29 or $2.99, the buyer could turn that purchase into *millions of dollars!* [Gold on this Earth was valued at a thousand times more than on Old Earth]. Any bank, jewelry company or large pawn shop would gladly pay millions of dollars for a gold bar the size of 12 pieces of PEZ Candy. Here was another titanic Change that also shocked the PEZ world: <u>All PEZ dispensers and candy were now sold from federal vending machines</u>. No customers touched the packages. No one could tell if a PEZ package was heavy or not heavy. Customers picked the new ones, and some old ones, from virtually unbreakable vending devices, found about everywhere.

The campaign was a huge success! Citizens that never bought PEZ before, bought PEZ now! Everyone did. Why not? A few bucks in coins into a machine, A-7 or G-8 pushed and maybe a Smokey the Bear-head dispenser dispensed *millions of dollars into your lap?*

Snake told Charles' head, *Now we can go back to PEZ Island and this will be at a point after the Golden Dispenser Campaign...*

Charlie was within earshot of others so he kept his communication to telepathy: *What's the difference?* he asked.

Snake replied, *Much more people, activity and Product out the door.*

Take me.

~~~

Reality changed. Charlie basically beamed (but not really) to the main tower in the very center of the #1 PEZ factory. Here was the largest producer of PEZ Candy and dispensers. Charlie was located at the heart of the Factory. It was a fabulous sight. There was almost too much color and motion and detail. *Look at this,* he said to himself. *FANTASTIC! Oh, the smell~~~*. Chuck's legs buckled when he took in a big whiff of air. The sweetness...*heavenly.* And overwhelming. He gained his composure in time.

You alright there, Charles? Snake chimed in with thoughts of concern.

Just fine. Now.

Chuck joined up with a tour group, learned more about the long/extended history of PEZ on this planet. Also, how it was exported off-world. He was amazed. Later, he broke from the group when Snake informed him of his appointment with the President of PEZ.

"The President of PEZ?" he blubbered to himself as the Devil entered an elevator that took passengers straight up to the lobby of the big man's office. His name was J.J. Martling (British, n.c.s.b.). One of his subordinates came up with the 'Golden Dispenser Campaign' and the "head" man wanted to capitalize on the mega idea as soon as possible. The huge question was: What new dispenser would be THE ONE? The one to hold gold and drastically change the life of an extremely fortunate buyer? It has not been decided yet. Mister Martling will choose. The suggestions were: a) One of the flying creatures from Avatar. b) The larger version of Grogu when he is older. 3) A redone Red Witch, like the first that was introduced to America. And 4) A black/Asian/female Santa Claus. The President had to choose one of the four today and could not decide. Problem.

A meeting with an outsider at this particular time

was out of the question. "Mister Martling cannot be disturbed." An appointment that should never have happened, happened.

"Charles Islington" was introduced and walked through the beautiful, wooden doors of Mister Martling's grand office. Unbelievable PEZ artwork and early paraphernalia hung on high walls. A gorgeous, round window let in golden sunlight that made everything shine.

The bearded President was an old gentleman, white hair. He spoke first. He said, "What can I do for you, Mister Islington?"

"It's what I can do for you, sir."

"And what is that, young man? Before you answer, I always like to ask: Where are you from?"

Charles blurted out the first town in his databased mind: "Ipswich."

"British, eh? Brother, no doubt. Jolly good. And what can you do for me?"

"Solve your problem at hand. I have the Golden Dispenser for you, right here, sir..." Mister Islington whipped out the Cat-head dispenser of his Queen that momentarily appeared as a Dog-head. But now it was back in its feline form...

"I love cats! Yes, I think you have something there, sir! We've done plenty of cats because I just love cats!"

"Hmmm." Charlie smiled. *It's going to work.*

President Martling said, "...But this one looks real! What's his name? Where's he from? The face almost rings a bell, eh?"

Charlie made up a good lie then planted the words in the President's head (spell) with a waved hand. "His name is Catwallender, from that Twilight Zone with the devil, one of them. Don't you remember the Devil was named after his cat in the show and this is the spittin' image of that particular cat? Hollywood's making a film of this TV show, even more reason to manufacture it. And who would expect, upon purchasing the PEZ with gold which would change a family's life completely, that it would come from a scary devil-cat called Catwallender? Isn't it perfect precision, sir?"

"Yes, I do remember! You know, that will fool absolutely everybody. My closest associates and Board members think it's one of the suggested four. Ah, but it won't be! My boy, you *have* solved a big problem for me in the nick of time! Mums the word. May I keep this?" The old man had a crazed look in his eyes.

Charlie went with the flow and answered, "You certainly may, sir. And I want no compensation whatsoever. Our secret is safe. I'll never tell which kind of dispenser has the gold. Simply knowing that I have contributed to your wonderful company in a small way gives me much satisfaction, Mister President, sir." He shook the President's hands.

"Good." Martling exhaled and then grabbed the cat dispenser. He felt a subtle vibration inside the plastic. He was totally absorbed by it, thoroughly mesmerized. He knew: As soon as next week, millions of Catwallenders will be shipped to every country on Earth and placed in federal vending machines. Charles was now ignored by the President.

Charles walked out of the room, silently. He made a successful pitch to the (parallel) President and was very pleased with himself. *The spell worked.*

TS Caladan

6. The Contest Winner

His name was Winston Jones. The whole planet knew the name: 'Winston Jones' immediately after the winner of the 'Golden Dispenser Contest' was announced. He lived in West McKeesport, Pennsylvania. That was where the vending machine (the President picked) was located and where the winner's family was located. Winston was a street-sweeper. He drove one of those large machines from midnight to 4AM and cleaned up trash left on side streets of West McKeesport. Mister Jones was no longer a street-sweeper. Now, he cleaned up in a different way. He was very rich.

The humble man made an emotional acceptance speech over Media that brought tears to the eyes of viewers. He was very, very sorry that he'd won and denied another family of incredible wealth. Winston plainly admitted to the world that he was given 17.5 million dollars for the gold bar by Sotheby's. [This was weird; they came to him and offered 17.5 million. How'd they know the winner before the news announced it? New winner Winston only understood that he had to sell the gold bar fast and took the first generous offer. The public and outsiders were left in the dark and no one questioned Sotheby's.].

The information was never let out to the general citizenry that Sotheby's held a private auction among Illuminati members and the first PEZ Gold Bar sold for **3.1 billion dollars**!! Why so high? PEZ was held in such great esteem that the barons, baronesses, dukes and duchesses thought PEZ gold bars could be *far more valuable in the future.* Here was the very first one. The holder of this Gold Bar could wield "mystical powers," they believed. Little did anyone realize that there will not be any more gold bars in vending machines in the years to come, as promised. There was no more Contest, but people thought that it continued and there would be more bars distributed in future. Even the royals were deceived. And who among commoners or among aristocratic devils, in their wildest dreams, would believe that the first bar, and what will happen later, were all produced by Satan?

Winston Jones secretly migrated his family to the island of Catalina and lived under a different name. Same as a Witness Protection Program. There, he bought a small sheep farm. They were isolated and lived in complete anonymity. His ten people, family and friends, lived happily on the beautiful island. His wife started a vineyard and they considered Wine as a business venture, but more of a hobby. Times were fabulous for the conservative 'Jones,' now 'Collins.' But only for the first year. Then, their secret got out of precisely who they were: HERE WERE THE BIG PEZ WINNERS! They changed their name to *Collins*. Winston admitted to his people on Catalina that their secret would get out, eventually. It was only a matter of time that someone in his group reached out to other family members in other parts of the country or the reverse happened. Someone snitched and now, through Social Media, everyone knew who they were and where they were. *Their lives became a nightmare!*

Rumors had grown that they received far more than 17 million dollars. [Untrue]. In fact, these good people refused to be part of big pay-out interviews or book deals. They did a couple tours with PEZ, but that was it. They refused to be public figures. Their wishes were respected. The family was not hounded by reporters in the beginning. And they hardly earned a penny outside of the cash they were originally handed. The Jones' didn't need money and took no later offers.

People camped out, just off of their property to look at them and record them with their phones. The family's sheep farm was invaded by a swarm of gawkers and reporters and people who recorded them on Social Media along with themselves. As if the citizens were a part of the story.

The Jones/Collins family on Catalina could not go outside of their home complex. They were followed. Always asked questions with phones shoved in their faces. All food was delivered and even some of the deliveries were faked by those who wanted to be inside their house to possibly get an exclusive interview. The children could not go to school. They realized that they had to leave the island and the happy life they had and once more relocate.

The family received some government assistance and were escorted to a private jet that swept them off to an undisclosed destination. But...

An unforeseen "accident" occurred, a major tragedy happened whereby the jet **exploded!** *Exploded into small pieces, 5 miles over the Pacific Ocean!*

The world was shocked. People around the planet were terribly saddened and held services for the dead and performed other displays of sorrow, regret and pain. The family certainly did not deserve what happened to them. From simple, hard-working people to great wealth and now they paid the ultimate price. The story broke the hearts of many and created such waves of tears, globally. The public felt violated. Social Media honored the Jones family, the same Internet that led to their demise.

Conspiracy Theorists had field days! Something sinister had to be behind the famous family's death. There always were horrible secrets behind big stories, the rich and famous, behind the little the public was handed over Media. What was true? Grocery magazine headlines, documentaries, YouTubes videos and talk shows buzzed with everything under the Sun: They were still alive and it was a plan from the beginning to give them complete sanctuary. Or: They were taken into space and partied with the likes of Prince, Michael Jackson and David Bowie. Or: Government sabotage, but why? Or: Sotheby's had them killed because the family was rumored to sue when they found out what the Gold Bar was really worth. Then, of course, the disaster could always have been caused by ALIENS. It's always aliens. Why? The theorists had to invent some reason that involved extraterrestrials. The best idea a few had was: All the signs were there for an alien invasion. This was an act of War, to hurt the human heart on a massive scale, and only the start of great destruction from the sky. Scientists had also predicted that some dramatic encounter was on the horizon and aliens would SHOW THEMSELVES for the first time in history.

What was the truth? Why did the government private jet really explode?

The truth? This time, unknown to everyone, some Conspiracy Theorists were correct. **This was an Act of War from outer space**. *Things to Come* would be a full-scale invasion by an alien species that are dark symbiotes. Human hosts to an inner snakelike species called Kull. The serpents wrapped around the human kundalini-energy of the spine. They assimilated humans. Humans were the only species with the right energy waves that fed the symbiote "worms."

Humans will lose the War. The invasion of Earth by very advanced aliens will change the few survivors into (basically) lifeless zombies, slaves, "things" with no independent freedoms or independent thoughts. It was the end of everything good and decent and human on Earth. But. The Kull invasion might not happen<>.

7. The Problem with New Dispensers

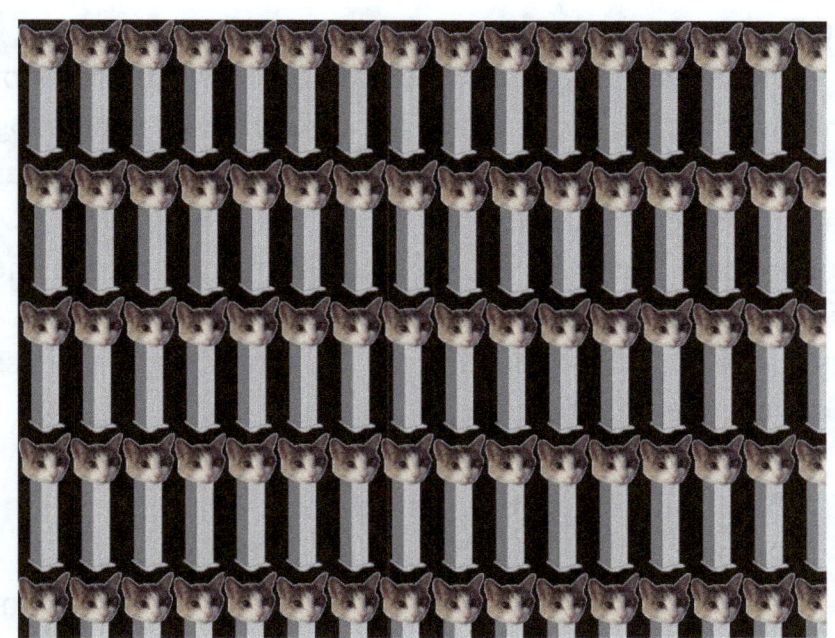

PREVIOUSLY:

"Don't you see the problem, sir?"

J.J. Martling was rather perplexed at the moment and did *not see* [Nazi] what his subordinate meant. Not at all. "Problem? I don't see a problem, James. These are the new dispensers, ready to be shipped to the four corners of the world, by God. Aren't the kitties little sweethearts? I love um, mmm."

"Yes, I love them too, sir. That's not what I was talking about, Mister President. I meant your 'Executive

Order Zed Zed 66.'"

J.J. cocked his head, stroked his white beard and remained befuddled. "Zed Zed 66 is as plain as the nose on your face, dear boy. The Order is as clear as a bell, a quartz crystal bell. What is your problem with Order 66?"

James was not sure what had come over the boss of this world's PEZ Company because he was not acting like himself, nor as if he had a sound mind. The man was more powerful than the U.S. president. The PEZ subordinate found it hard to find the words, broach the subject or to express even a hint of criticism. He gave it a try: "Well sir, look...you are ordering endless Catwallender dispensers..."

"Wonderful! What is wrong with that, James?"

"Well sir, there are no others?"

"Wot?"

"There won't be any more new and different dispensers. You're ordering the termination of, of, of, *Christ,* of any more new and different models! SIR! PEZ won't be putting out different designs or old designs anymore. Only, and I mean *only,* the Catwallender dispenser, sir. May I please ask you...why, oh, why you've come to this big decision, President Martling, sir?"

"That's easy..." He stared down and stroked the furry head of the original dispenser Mister Islington gave to him. "When you've found the best, there's no sense in the rest. Hi, my love. I want the world to see just how beautiful you are, my Catwallender. Yes, that's right, my girl. I couldn't possibly put out an inferior product now, now that there is...*you* in the world, now could I?" J.J. turned and his glazed eyes looked into the face of his underling. He asked him, sincerely, "Don't you agree, James?"

James was frozen and then he shook a little. His thoughts were sensible, logical, sane and crystal clear: *People loved the dispensers for the variations in heads! DA! The business would STOP! Collecting won't be collecting if they were all the same. The collections that everyone collects! The conventions that almost everyone attended, passionately! What will happen if PEZ Company, only and forever, manufactured to the world one type of head?? The result must be, must be, the eventual end of the largest and by far the most successful company on Earth! Aaaaaaaaaaaaaaaaah!!!*

"Don't you agree, James?"

He finally uttered a response: "Of course, sir."

TS Caladan

8. "It's a Lovely Day in the Neighborhood"

More *magical* benefits flowed from the crumpled Fabrini Multi-Pass: There were big "stipends" attached and Charlie was able to afford a cute, little cottage. He chose a quiet college-town near Lake Erie called 'Edinboro,' spelled differently than the esteemed, British university: Edinborough. Snow had covered the ground, as it did much of the year. Charlie was unfamiliar with snow and wanted to experience it. Far back into the foggy recesses of his database, he recalled a lifetime where he knew cold/white snow very well. But that existence was almost totally blotted out, like only small fragments of a dream.

The demon was an attractive man, an attractive *young* man, compared to his ancient dark soul and his dark past. *He had hair!* Brown hair in a medium length. He decided for the rest of his time here on this low-tech planet, he'd bury his distant past 100%. He'd forget his vampire-ish beginnings where he devoured prey after prey and drank their blood. That person was long gone now. Charlie regretted all the terrible things he'd done and was forced to do. This was a new planet, a new galaxy and a new beginning for the *man.*

Charlie acted human. He didn't need to sleep, but he

slept in a soft bed. He ate good food and tasted delicious drinks, although he didn't need to do that either. He still was an electric iso Monitor 'under the skin.' He didn't know why but he chose a flesh face similar to tennis pro: Carlito Alcaraz, (from database) only he made sure to never play the game and confuse anyone who watched. The man walked among young people in the small town and no one suspected *he was not of this world.*

It was a warm day in Edinboro, an unusually warm day. No Snow. *The town's "Think Snow" banner worked its magic days ago,* the man thought...but not on this day of sunshine and 75 degrees. Charlie walked through leaves on the ground and made his way to the town's old graveyard, next to an adorable lake. Most people bypassed the gravestones that went back to the 1700s and enjoyed the lake with a homemade beach 20-feet long. Not Chuck. The gravestones fascinated him. He touched them. *Why did I come here?* It was like he buried his own past. He was alone and sat among the stones and tried *meditation.* What was he to do now that fate brought him to this place? Maybe there'd be an answer?

Snake placed a thought into his brain: *Check out your dispenser collection. You'll find something very interesting has happened. You don't have to walk back home. I'll just move you to a half hour later. Here we go><.*

A second later...

He was there. Back home in his clean cottage on Mill Street. It remained a lovely day in the neighborhood and Charlie was very anxious to find out what Snake meant. Was his collection, which he loved, going to shed light on the next task that he must perform?

He had a beautiful corner display case and that's where his terrifically swell collection was stored. The case had two curved glass doors and black shelves and great lighting. The problem was: He didn't have many dispensers. Charlie caught the collecting bug way too late. He wasn't going to win the Gold Bar or even be close to having the most dispensers in the world. In fact, his collection was extremely pathetic. It consisted of Darth Vader, Boba Fett, the Deathstar, Vampire, Witch, Kro, Wario, Ghost, a One-Eye Minion and the Joker. He only had 10! But it was a start.

Snake spoke aloud: *"Hey Chucky, take them out of the case and put them on the table..."*

"Hey! Stop telling me what to do?! Okay? I hate that! Who made you boss? Who died and left you King?" The man was very upset for the moment.

"But you asked me what you should do?" Snake replied, innocently.

"Oh yeah." He stroked his chin. "Ah. Yeah, well. Maybe I don't like yer attitude?"

"You sure kiss the Queen's ass."

"HEY! By the way, is there any way we can separate? I mean...permanently?"

"No. I'm like a symbiote. Take it up with Queeny; I don't make the rules, hon."

"Now. What's this about my collection?" Charlie said as he obeyed commands and placed each of the dispensers in a row on the table, all 10.

Snake replied, *"For one, isn't it odd these particular ones gravitated to you, or the other way around?"*

"Whatchu mean?" Charlie blindly asked.

"Look at them. They're all nasty villains and bad things! I'm surprised LeBron James and Mickey Mouse aren't there too, eh? Ha..."

"Wot? I think they're cool."

"You would."

"I don't see what yer getting at, where we're going, what's this have to do with...?"

"Well, ya have a little surprise coming, my man. That's where I'm going with this."

"What?"

The voice in his head said: *"Look behind you, next to the sofa. Your special package came today...the one you're dying to get? It's here!"*

The man and former Beast became Pleased as Punch! "It's really here? 'Bout time!"

"You sure 've been spending money on that holy pass of yours. Gee, it's like magic. How much these New Dispensers from the PEZ Company set you back?"

Charles did not answer. He ripped through the well-sealed package and could not wait to get his hands on what was inside of this very, very, special package from PEZ Island. He did not see that Snake had physically MATERIALIZED on the table in perfect alignment and next to the others as #11. Charlie grabbed what were the latest dispensers from the Company, the ones on special order. He was ecstatic! He couldn't wait to place them with the others and later fill out his splendid display case. But...

When he returned to the table, he saw the dispenser with the Dog-head next to the Joker and screamed: *"Aaaaugh!"*

"Relax. It's me. Ha, ha. You are the wimpiest devil I've ever seen, HA!"

"I don't know that word, but I'm sure it's not a compliment..."

"Ha."

"Wait. You're the Queen's dispenser that I left with Mr. Martling? How...?"

Snake moved her head and stated: *"Original that he possesses is not the original. It's a duplicate. I'm the first one. Why the head flipped over to the Dog-form, I don't know.*

"Ah. So now I can call you a bitch?"

"Hilarious. I'm gettin' to love our banter, Chucky. Why don't you line up all the new ones you received right along with us, eh? Yeah, you can start putting them next to me, #12, #13, #14 and so on, aye?"

"Okay." The man did so robotically, carefully,

gently, and without much thought. The 40 "new dispensers" were laid out with the other 11, which made a grand total of 51. Charlie was so proud once he got them in perfect position and knew they'd appear far more spectacular when placed in the case. For now, the view was overwhelming: *He had 51 PEZ dispensers!!*

The Dog-head told him, nicely, *"Please take a seat, take your shoes off, relax. Here's a drink."* A glass of cold raspberry lemonade suddenly appeared on the table.

Charlie drank. Smiled again and said, "Aaaaah." Then, he stared at his collection.

Strange Interlude~.

Snake asked: *"Now...what's wrong with this picture?"*

After about ten frozen seconds, Charlie twisted and turned his head and expressed: *"Oh.* Oh, you mean that there's 11 different dispensers and 40 Catwallenders?"

Snake responded with one word: *"Yeeeeeah."*

9. *Maxine*

All over the Earth, in every country, people (almost every solitary person) collected PEZ dispensers. But they were under a magical spell and did **not see** that all of them had physically changed to the Catwallender-head. It was collectively fine and accepted. It went *unseen* by everyone. The powerful Spell caused a bizarre oddity: Earthlings acted as if the dispensers *were* different. As if there were microscopic variations in new models, as always, but there weren't any differences in the Catwallenders.

Inside PEZ vending machines, new PEZ packages appeared as usual and took the places of ones that sold. Each had a different number on them, but they were all the SAME head. Citizens just adored the furry cat-heads, each and every furry cat-head that this parallel Company produced.

The public continued as they had always done: bought/sold and traded collections and dispensers. They held conventions where people proudly displayed their collections, used the Internet and sold small numbers or large numbers of Catwallender dispensers. The fascination was no longer the *differences* between dispenser heads, no, it was simply a numbers game.

People were very excited by just seeing massive numbers of the Cat dispensers shown in one place, but **lost the ability to appreciate differences in PEZ dispensers and in people.**

Everything was different now. Everything was the same. How could people on Earth NOT REMEMBER that PEZ dispenser heads were different? How could they have forgotten the bright colors and different colors of the stem pedestals? Now, all the pedestals were gray. Colorless. The wide variety of individual dispensers in personal collections was Everything! No mas. They were all the same, but people acted as if nothing was out of the ordinary. PEZ paraphernalia also changed. In the past, images on various PEZ products showed different character-heads and different thing-heads. But today, a different history happened and every shred of PEZ products always displayed the same face: The face of a cat, supposedly, from a Twilight Zone program.

Later...

"Chucky, Chucky, what are you doing?!" the Dog-head dispenser on the table shouted at the man in his living room. Charlie moved furniture from one room and placed them in another. *"Come here. I want to talk to you."*

"I'm busy."

"Okay. I see what the problem is here. And an instant solution has formulated in my digital mind.

Hmmm."

"What?" Charlie asked. He heard little of the dispenser's words. He decided to stop his task at hand and he approached the table. "What are you squawking about, pest?"

"I've decided on a new look and a new name."

"Huh? *You* decided?"

"I want something different, something that I chose, something MOBILE! That's the ticket, my man. I'm under orders to be stuck to you like glue. But, screw your head and seeing through your eyes! Your eyes. Always you, huh? What about me? I wanna function out here in the physical world, see? Bye Snake. I imagined a 'floating orb' - it just came to me, eh? A floating, white orb...yes? Can't you see it, Charlie? I can...and now, I AM..."

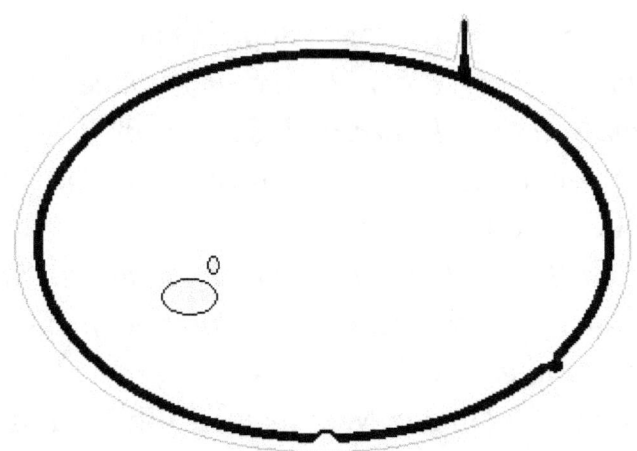

Charlie jumped at the sight of a 2-foot long spheroid that suddenly *popped* into existence about 5 feet above the hardwood floor~. The Queen's Cat and pedestal were gone.

"I'm floating, I'm floating!" the digital Program sang at the top of her audio 'lungs.'

The man ran his hand through his brown hair and was delighted. He chuckled. His close companion was happy. *How nice.*

"So whatja think, man? You know, of the new look?" the excited orb asked.

Charlie replied, "Kind of spartan, isn't it?"

"You are right, buddy. I'll work on cool details later. Hey! I can fly!!" The orb *zoomed* out of a closed window in a flash and did not break it. She vibrated through it. She was gone and Charlie was left alone.

"That's funny. Now what? Hey, dude, I mean *Lady!* This is sticking close to me like glue? Where are you? And, what? You want a new name?"

His close companion zapped back in. *"Chuck! Everything is fine! I can break time/space so seconds away from you are like hours. It's Heaven!"*

"Yer sounding more like Queen Zep. Oh, and now what do I call you?"

"Alright! I've thought about this long and hard and have decided on: Maxine. Call me Maxine, just don't call me late for dinner, ha."

"Maxine, eh? Okay. Maxine it is. Why Maxine?"

"It's like cat-names. You don't give 'm names, they telepathically tell you what they want to be called. I mean, who'd ever come up with 'Mister Snarflefeather'

*or 'Wankerson Beebop,' eh? Maybe the Great Queen or
Great King in the sky decreed 'Maxine' for me? Who
knows?"*

"As far as I'm concerned yer 'gettin' too big for your
britches,' says the saying. Okay, the idea is: Yer gonna
follow me everywhere? Shite. Just don't be a bloody
nuisance, I mean, any *more* of a nuisance than you've
already been...Maxine!"

"Won't even notice I'm here..."

"Oh, joy."

TS Caladan

10. The Effect

"You don't know that you, you catalyst, DID THIS! If not for you and the forces behind you, this would never have happened. See, now I'm talkin' sense, aye?"

"Did what?"

"Check out your collection now, why don't you?" the Maxine orb suggested.

Charlie took a second look at all 50 of his precious dispensers and the "villains and bad things" had changed to Catwallenders. At the present moment and for every moment in the future, they will stay Catwallenders.

"Wow. I saw the change."

"I'll tell you, in every country, this has happened again and again. Millions of avid collectors that have collected for most of their lives...they can't see the differences anymore. Their vast collections are all the same now, and they're proud of it. They can't wait to add one more Catwallender to all the other Catwallenders they've collected.

"That's terrible!"

"I know," Maxine responded with much pride in her voice. *"You are one of the very fortunate ones, Charlie. Aaaah, maybe not? To see both sides of the 'mirror.' You'll remember the Darths and Bobo Fetts and single-*

eyed Minions, and the other heads. But they won't. The whole planet will be Bird Boxed..."

"What?"

"Look it up. It means: blinded. They'll think nothing of it; there wouldn't have been any changes to them. They'll think it's always been that way. Anyhoo..."

"WHY? Maxine, I still do not have a total picture of what we're doing, what you've told me so far, what that means? So what? We've changed these little toys; we've hypnotized Earthlings to not see the changes. Why? *This is evil??* Ha, ha. If I made Bombs I would do more damage! Is this ZEP's joke on me, her biggest fool and Dog!? I don't get it. They still LOVE their collections! So what if they can't see it?"

"Dude, I'm smarter than you, I can see further down 'the road' than you, and I don't get it. But I'm starting to, as more pieces appear on the path. Let me explain. I can show you in real pictures of what has just started to happen and will continue to steamroll from now on on Earth. I can display for you your EFFECT. Yes?"

"My Effect? You're going to connect everything together like at the end of a Who-Done-It movie? How ya gonna do that?" Charlie inquired.

"A Magic Screen. Viola!"

Suddenly, a very big screen 156 inches long appeared and hovered in midair.

Maxine explained that they could view true events on Earth, today, in real time, or yesterday, or jump ahead into the future. *"But, if I do that, my friend. WE also jump with the changes, into tomorrow or whenever..."*

"Great! Let's fast forward and show me the EFFECT, you called it." Charlie saw that another of his favorite drinks was tableside, so he took a swig. He smiled.

"Here we go." The white spheroid bobbed up and down more than usual. *"Oh wait, let's go into the Past first with the Time Machine, for an important reason: This Darkening, this Blackening, of society, everything being literally pushed/forced to the Dark Side has been happening for many decades prior to your arrival, Chief. Much more subtly. Your Effect simply shoved everything over the edge and plunged it into pure Hell. Mordor. That's Things to Come; we have to wait for that. Screen, show him some of the first changes that occurred to human society as part of this sinister Plan set in place by the leaders of Earth..."*

The view screen showed cars, freeways, the fast movements of vehicles, crowded lanes of automobiles and different kinds of trucks. The wide picture took up the full screen with a montage of moving vehicles.

"What are you showing me?" Charlie asked.

"This was 20 years ago and it is pretty much the same today, right?"

"Okaaaay, this is some early Effect of Evil?"

Maxine explained that, *"Long ago, gas-combustion engines should have and could have been outlawed, banned, never used again. Many different kinds of power sources could have been utilized to motivate crafts, such as quartz crystals, hemp, water, Tesla towers and even lightspeed beaming was possible! Evil corporate heads, Kings and Queens, do not share power or technology. The Royals did numerous acts to halt progress for the people. It's quite staggering if one researched 'Suppressed Technology.' So, you're not going to get the good stuff, as you should have long ago."*

Charlie heard those words by Maxine, closely. When she said "you," he took that to mean *him:* that he was a member of the human race. Charlie smiled in awe.

"Here, take a look at what society could have been..."

The screen displayed a big, bright city and the view was something out of a sci-fi movie. Streams of fantastic air-vehicles filled the sky! There were pyramids in the distance. There were a few floating cities on the horizon! Spectacular! Wondrous!

Charlie's mouth opened, his eyes enlarged. He asked her: "What year is that?"

She replied, *"1980."*

One timeline frazzled and scrambled Chuck's database. "1980? Really?"

"There was a Hollywood film called 'Just Imagine' in 1930 and it projected what life on Earth would be like in 50 years. Saucers flew and cops pulled speeders over in mid flight. Planned marriages, test-tube babies,

global-Media, etc. Here's what I'm getting at, the real deal of what happened in another universe..."

The screen changed again. Maxine declared, *"Now just imagine...Here's what the world, the way it was going, should have looked like only 20 years ago..."*

The view was the same montage in the beginning with freeways and changes of perspective to other urban freeways. The cars were drastically different, though. They were colorful. They were small. They had big rubber bumpers. No vehicles were gray. White and black were rarities among car colors. Few trucks, and they were colorful. She explained: *"More than 90% were perfected, <u>electric</u> vehicles and the rest were a combination of various solar-powered vehicles. **Gasoline-combustion engines were against Federal Law!** You couldn't even play with gas engines in rural areas. Environmentalists made sure of that. People lost their love of cars, in time. But here in this world of today, there was 'Fast and Furious 11!'"*

The screen changed to: Floors of houses, floors of apartment buildings, floors of offices and the floors of just about any place where people gathered.

"I'm clueless, Maxie. Yer showing me *floors?"*

"Yes. There's a connection...just wait for it. What do you see on the floors?"

"They're hardwood floors," Charlie described.

Maxine's response was: *"Here's what floors should look like..."*

The screen transitioned to WALL-to-WALL CARPETS. Thick, deep blue carpets, dark purple carpets and thick, comfortable, soft, luxurious, magnificent, brown carpets. They actually extended from one wall to another wall. All the floors had wall-to-wall carpets in a montage of beautiful interiors.

Charlie tried to wrap his head around Maxine's point. He pulled on his hair and rubbed the side of his human head. "Textures!? Soft compared to hard? Yes?"

"Now you're getting it, brother. The Not Sees that control this, all of it, have socially engineered this and much more for Evil purposes, which I will show you. They've also made killer-cigarettes more fashionable than they've ever been before."

"Intriguing. Do go on." He finished his lemonade.

"...Human children should grow up within soft environments. Feng shui. Environments have an Effect on people. It's proven that hard environments cause humans to be hard, cold, rigid, and even heartless/cruel people. But if environments were soft and cozy and comfortable, then, the Effect tends to make them soft, fuzzy, warm, cuddly, good people. THEY don't want that. They want you violent, at war and at each other's throats! One of many ways to do that is...throw rugs and hard floors."

"So that's where the rainforests went?"

"Yep."

The screen displayed infant children with small cats on a nice, thick, shag rug.

"Aaaw. *Kitties*. How cute is that?" Charlie expressed, with emotion. [Was the former Beelzebub a real human now? The scene melted his sudden heart].

Then the screen shifted to an alternate reality. The very same infants and kittens were in the same room, only the scene contained hardwood floors.

"That's just not right. Rugs are better. Soft is better. There's traction. Quieter. No slipping. Should be rugs, I mean if humans cared about their children and kitties?"

"Well, Chucky, hardwood floors have been decreed by the Royals to be everywhere. And they are. All new apartment building floors now must go wood, when previously it was cheap rugs. Rooms that were carpeted are now hardwood. In movies or commercials on TV or the Internet, you will never see wall-to-wall carpets anymore. It's one evil mother-fucking plan that citizens are completely unaware of..."

"Huh."

"If the neo-Nazis that control Earth had their way, people would be living on IRON floors. Sig Heil."

"Where'd you get these emotions, lady? Don't answer. Any more?"

"Lots. Look at clothes and color."

The large screen showed another montage: groups of people from the 1950s. They were rock 'n rollers and beatniks. Elvis. There was no color and teenagers were rougher/violent, the first movement post-WW2. Then pushed/forced were the Beatles, Beatlemania, the British invasion of America, psychedelics and **COLOR**! Peace and Love. Woodstock, Altamont and music festivals at the time. *Color* was everywhere, on posters, on people. Everything changed from black and white to bright colors.

"Yes. It was very different in color years later. And attitudes changed."

"This was the British Plan all along. They control all music, the arts, TV, cinema, sports, politics, the nukes, the planet's armies, world-religions, the world's money, you name it. Royals are Social Engineers and they do this to keep control, to keep in power. They plan everything many years in advance. Fascists have made everybody a dystopian who loves their enslavement. Look at the screen, Charles..."

The scene advanced to the early 1990s.

"We've completely skipped over Punks, Grunge, and the Decline of Western Civilization. Back then ('90) and today, it's Rap music, the only type of music that is unmercifully pushed and pushed again. Good, talented musicians and real Music have been cancelled in the new world. Rap is the 'undying monster' that will now NEVER go away! A Destroyer of Music. Styles used to change. No more cycles. Devo. Stagnation. Rap should be spelled 'Wrap.' Access: 'Wrap party, things are wrapped up when done and finished' and so are we. I mean the way Earthlings are heading...

"Wrap. Yes, I see what you mean, Maxine. No more

singing."

"Note the color or lack of? No color. Back to BLACK. It means something. People, and really it's the youth, that are so influenced by Sound and Vision..."

Charlie commented, "No more peace and love, eh? Back to the color of beatniks and the first rockers in leather with slicked-back hair."

"Speaking of hair, HAIR is a very important part of this. It means something."

"Explain."

"Hair has always meant freedom and strength. Hair is protein/power. Long hair has always meant Strength. Access: 'Sampson.' Kings and commoners in Medieval times had long hair. It was Britain's World Wars where we first saw short-cropped hair as an accepted style for society. Short hair and BALDNESS has always meant slavery, servitude, certainly not freedom. Access: Tibetan monks who all wear the same orange uniforms, which correspond to orange uniforms of inmates in prisons. What else do they have in common? Baldness. Why are all dudes on Earth in beards? Media has pushed this. No individualism any more. Bearded barbarians."

"M, yer sayin': Royal dictators who run everything have set up a world of slave-subjects, who are devoted to them, and who do not know they are slaves?"

"Yes. They've been given campaigns of 'Empowerment,' which is a joke."

"Alright, I'm seeing Light. The Effect that didn't

start with me has made them black and white in their hearts and souls. Colorless like the cars, clothes, stories, etc. I've accessed their music, movies and TV and what a gigantic difference over time..."

"People are given pure crap today: the worst stories, movies, shows, TV, ads, celebrities, everything! The worst technology, but the youth have been trained to believe 'this is the best.' Charles, I'm trying to relay that the total darkness and contrived fear in the air now as well as Social Media have made the general public Zombies. Access: 'Walking Dead.' The youth are the walking dead now and they don't have a clue. This was the original intention: to make you cold and robotic."

"I see. Who can see the Big Picture when they've dumbed-down everyone? All the connections and how they've changed things over time. Okay...PEZ. Our whole assignment here on Earth and what we did changing dispensers? I don't..."

Maxine replied, *"On this planet, collecting dispensers is a passion. We pushed that to a far greater degree with the Gold Bar and their belief in a Gold Bar. But the SAMENESS of the collections, all the same Catwallenders. Don't you see? <u>They ignore the sameness of the dispensers and they ignore the fact that everyone has been molded into the same creature.</u> Pushed in the wrong/single direction. Show 'm."*

View screen visually presented the typical dude of the 2020s. He was a "suede-head" (almost bald) covered in tattoos, and dressed in black. This was a person that did not care. A person who was never trained or educated well. A young man whose potential will never be realized in such dark times. A youth that wore chains and a cross and devil-stars or skull-images as fashion statements. The young man on the screen smoked cigarettes and did not care and thought it was cool. Millennials, for the most part, do not care. They subconsciously know the State has lied to them and do not care about them. Why should they care? Why should they if families and friends, down deep, don't care anymore? Why, if nearly every movie and show [brainwashing] showed insanity/nonsense and pushed bad behaviors? They used to care and people treated people with true respect in that other timeline long gone.

The screen displayed a typical young *woman* of the new century, and...

Charlie gagged. She was dressed dark. The last thing she appeared like was feminine. Was beauty now lean and mean? Girls were violent, tranny warriors? Again, *girls* smoked cigarettes (not pot) and they were covered in hideous tattoos?

"I've seen enough." Charlie's words made the screen turn off. It was black.

"You might want to view one more video, my man," the white orb suggested.

"Play it." Charlie was disgusted and sad. He played a large part in the *Decline of Human Civilization.* "Why am I not happy? I should be elated? This will thrill the Queen. I mean, *Christ,* her Big Plan seems to be a raging success, aye? What's this?"

The screen came on and showed a future timeline, one particular Thing to Come. Maxine left the man alone to contemplate the moving images in front of him.

A beautiful, young couple in fantastic colors and in futuristic clothes entered their mini-spaceship built for two. It was 1980. In the background was a super Metropolis. The young boy and girl laughed and knew the safe adventure that laid ahead of them. They were happy and in love. They sealed themselves in, kissed for good luck and blasted off to the stars! Lovelier and lovelier...

Charlie perked up, noticeably. He pumped himself up as if he had *faith.* He saw something he thought he'd never see. He felt like he had two hearts. He cried.

11. "The Fake Alien Invasion"

Five decades ago, there was a secret/federal Plan to fake an alien invasion.

Why not deceive the people one more time? It could be easily done with covert tech that had been hidden from the general public. The logic went like this: *As we have faked World Wars and produced every bit of awesome destruction, damage and death that went with the chaos as well as made artificial "natural disasters" and "social wars on the street"...we could do the same with a bogus alien invasion. As we've faked 9/11 and created a false enemy that we utterly manipulated...we could do the same with an alien invasion that everyone believed. WE ARE THE NME! We are the only Enemy to humankind! Outsiders will never discover that WE orchestrated an invasion that we completely controlled. Same as how we arranged for the invasion of the Ukraine, while outsiders all think puppet-Russia was to blame. We will become the New Enemy and wage WAR and will rain terror down from the skies! No one will ever know the truth because they believe exactly what **we** force them to believe~~~.*

Whoever thought that the Third World War would be fought against Aliens? You mean the movies were right? All the programming Hollywood had presented like 'War of the Worlds' and 'Earth vs. The Flying Saucers' and 'Independence Day' were true and accurately predicted that this would occur in the real world?

If the invasion was fake: How could international scientists, funded by Britain, have pulled off such a worldwide deception? Answer: Holograms from satellites that round the clock orbited the Earth. Particle Beam weapons from space on the order of intense LASERS could actually poke holes through the planet! That is, if the Illuminati so desired? They pushed anything and everything over Media, according to their Agenda. A *War of the Worlds* and a great Fear Campaign from such a catastrophic event could be easily created and spread over Media.

For decades, Conspiracy Theorists were in place and were prepared to deny the validity of any alien invasion. No matter what destruction happened on Earth, they would be united, stand together and express to the world: Aliens were *not* involved. These were terrorist acts that were planned and executed by the throne of England. In the present situation of 2023, the Conspiracy Theorists were 100% dead WRONG.

What actually happened fooled teams of scientists as well as royal fascists. **The alien invasion was not faked. It was a real invasion.**

The world went to war on Christmas Day of 2023!

Newspaper headlines from every country on Earth declared: **WAR!** We had been attacked on Christmas Eve, a horrible tragedy that no one had thought possible: *Mount Everest EXPLODED!!* The force was so incredibly powerful that a titanic crater remained after all the ash, debris and dust had fallen. *Thousands of human beings had died by one push of a button from a ship in space* and the finger that pushed it was a human finger. A human finger which was guided by an alien symbiote wrapped around a human's kundalini energy.

The next big plot-point in a true alien invasion came when Earth's Radio Telescopes all received a *message* from the enemy! The initial thoughts of the Powers That Be were to cover up the message and keep it sealed from the public's eyes and ears. The leaders soon discovered that was impossible. Therefore, "They" released the English words that were composed by the Kull exactly as they were broadcast through the large arrays of radio telescopes. The Kull told the people of Earth:

"Months ago, we destroyed a federal jet because it held a well-known and beloved family. Purpose: to create extreme sadness in human hearts, globally. On your Christmas Eve, we conducted our second Act of War and destroyed the tallest peak on your planet, also beloved. The mountain was of special interest to others off-Earth and, therefore, the reason for its removal. We are the Kull! To your leaders: We demand

your planet's unconditional surrender to our forces! If in 24 hours, we do not receive a reply of total surrender on a 7 and a half hertz-wave frequency, our A.I. has chosen your continent of Australia to be annihilated. End message."

12. Who are the Kull?

The Kull have been portrayed in a number of Hollywood movies forced upon humans, such as: Klingons, the Borg, the Goa'uld, the Trill, Flash Gordon drones and other dual or symbiotic lifeforms. Secret Masters of Earth have known of two groups of mighty aliens in space that were virtually our Overseers: The large, 2-legged Lizards (television's Gorn) and the Kull, militaristic human-host species with a *snake* inside them. Lizards have owned the Earth, legally, for millions of years. The only reason the Kull have not attacked the human home planet previously was because of a treaty with the Lizards. News in the Solar System and unknown to billions on Earth: *The Lizards were leaving* and were done with this fucked-up planet that they have drained, used up. With the Lizards gone, this allowed their enemy Kull to come in and be the 'new Sheriff in town.' What had been portrayed in fiction...was not fiction.

Why not simply wipe out the human infestation on the planet's surface via poisons, bombs, phasers or photon torpedoes? (They're real too). The Kull did not want to damage the new planet that could add to their vast Empire. They wanted to find out how it could be utilized for their purposes. What valuable minerals Earth still possessed and what could the Kull do inside of Earth's hollow interior?

Humans had to go. The message and terms of surrender were a means for people to not resist, to willfully not take up arms and be eventually herded like cattle into destruction chambers. The best human specimens would be assimilated as hosts by the Kull to increase their numbers.

The secret leaders of the planet were so frightened when they realized Their Reign Was Over, their ruthless rule had come to a bloody end, that they...

Surrendered. A human reply to the aliens was broadcast on a 7 and a half hertz wavelength. The message primarily stressed *mercy*. The words hoped the aliens would be merciful to the "innocent children of Earth." [irony].

The New World under the reign of Kull was a world of FEAR. People streaked headlong into madness for decades. Today, streets were empty. Cities were depopulated with few that remained. They left after a 'Great Purge,' where many died and suffered terribly because of starvation and insane/vicious gangs of survivors.

Pez 4 Ever

One human, out of thousands of humans that was spared *the Purge,* was named Jeffrey Janes. He was a young, amateur tennis player, an up-and-comer. But that was in the old world, before the Kull. Today was a different story. Jeffrey was assimilated because of his youth and strength. He no longer had a name. He was no longer human. He was #1701-794. He was only a hulk, a skin, an empty android, 'robotoid,' basically a *vehicle* for an intelligent species of snakelike conquerors. One of the top Kull 'pilots' maneuvered the man as it also fed off of him.

Jeff and thousands of humans had been assimilated. Mindless drones with no will of their own when under 'the influence.' They obeyed the will of the *snake* inside. Like an arm or leg had no independent will and only moved because of electrical impulses from the brain, the same could be said of Kull drones.

1701-794 performed a variety of physical tests which demonstrated the piloting skills of the 'driver.' Kull officials were pleased with the tests on the man who used to be Jeffrey Janes. The aliens understood that one of their best pilots operated a strong specimen and they expected amazing results because of the union.

1701-794 was in 'hibernation,' also called 'cold storage' or in 'idle mode.' The Kull snake rested or slept, which meant the human just stood there, motionless. He was nude and in perfect line with other host specimens who were also nude. It was a 'resting spot' for Kull who, for an odd reason, slept near others. The healthy, strong and mindless humans aligned only an inch away from the next mindless human. They all looked out in one direction and with the same blank expression on their faces.

Why did the aliens have the humans align together during their rest period? The answer was quite surreal: The worms, the snakes, the Kull serpents, lived a dual life themselves. They were *Dream Weavers*. In the real/physical world, they were only ugly/slithering snakes. But in their **dreams**, they could be anything they wanted to be and do anything they wanted to do. These hideous creatures and mass-killers in the material world were, *in dreams, lovely beings who loved and existed in big/bright beautiful dimensions of fantastic things!* They interacted with souls of their kind in tenderness and as other species in phenomenal and very colorful fantasies.

But. *Dreams were dreams and the real/physical world was the real/physical world.* The two did not meet for the Kull. Did the aliens have to be evil in the physical world? Did they have to offset what wondrously, magically appeared in their dreams? Maybe the idea was: Such devilish horrors and terrors in the real world might produce the most extraordinary and phenomenal visions in their Dream Worlds? Possibly. Nevertheless, their objective was to wreak all the havoc they could in the universe that Lucifer fell into. They were going to be as BAD AS IT GETS!

Pez 4 Ever

1701-794 stood there with the other hosts in a line, mindless, void and vacant, until ordered to respond by an impulse of energy. He felt like a statue, a doll, a puppet, something plastic, without the smallest trace of warmth and life. He was as all the rest, the same as a clone. An entity without individuality. Another 'brick in the wall' and 'bozo on the bus.' The same. He didn't want to be like everyone else. He wanted to be different. He was an individual in his heart and in his soul and in his blood. 1701-794 should not have had *thoughts,* independent thoughts or a sense of Self, but he did. Sometimes miracles happened~.

He remembered. He knew his name that the aliens wiped. *Jeffrey.* He remembered the invasion! Earthlings surrendered completely. The Kull destroyed Australia anyway, as a show of ominous power, to prove they were *gods among men!*

Jeffrey Janes remained perfectly still and in perfect line with the others of his kind, but there had been a significant change. His brain became unwiped for some odd reason. Tremendously strong thoughts flowed into his skull and he actually *felt* that he could move. He felt and had warm feelings. Jeffrey tried to move and a finger may have twitched. Then, the former 1701-794 felt the dark, ugly 'thing," curled up in his lower chest. It felt like a black, greasy rock of hard shit in his gut and he wanted it out. *It still slept!* He knew. If he could only move, he might be able to rip it out? But he couldn't move. Not yet. It wasn't a matter of prayer, it was a matter of sheer will. More sharp/clear thoughts came into his brain and along with them came POWER...

He moved. He definitely moved his arm and waved it ever so slightly. More strength streamed through his veins. His breathing increased. Jeffrey Janes knew he could move his whole body now that some outside Voice told him to: "ACTIVATE!" The athletic man grabbed hold of the cold rail that the humans stood behind. He concentrated and used all the strength he could muster. *The rail broke!* The recoil from the violent action woke the monster wrapped around Jeff's spine! The creature uncurled and was ready to regain 100% control of his body when...

Jeffrey grabbed the bent rail and impaled himself on it! The Kull serpent screamed in pain! It did not expect a steel rail plunged into its head, certainly not after the pretty pictures it experienced during sleep. It was dead.

Janes was a bloody mess, but he was alive and FREE. He shoved his hand into the open wound and pulled out the symbiote. He threw the dead snake as far as he could. His hand put pressure on the hole. He looked around for anything that helped. He was one of twelve young people along the rail. *Why didn't the other Kulls wake after all the commotion?* Jeff figured they were in a deeper sleep phase. Just now, he noticed that one of the humans on the end was wearing clothes, a pretty girl. His first thought was: *Did the Kull-snake want a vehicle that looked like a princess?*

He staggered to his feet and got a better view. He was inside a large round room. No door. There was an archway that led to some other part of the ship. *I guess, Kull had no need for locked doors on a ship they totally controlled?* A helpful thought struck Janes' fine mind. Fate? *Maybe she's clothed for a reason?* The man bled more and more and had to stop the flow soon. He tore off strips of the *princess'* long gown without disturbing her body. He found the bandages he desperately needed. The thick strips were wrapped tightly around his body and the blood stopped.

"Whew!"

Then he looked down the line at his comatose mates, 6 guys and 5 gals. There weren't many human beings anymore. And what was left of them were robot-slaves. One more thought entered his brain, a way to save them and make them free also. Jeffrey snapped off a small section of the rail. He moved farther away from the line and banged the metal pipe on the hard floor. He thought the noise might bring others to the room, but it didn't. One end of the 'weapon' was sharpened. With it, he *gouged* every one of his people in the right spot to kill their symbiote>. There was enough cloth in the pretty girl's long train (gown) that it patched all 12 wounds.

They lived. [Just Imagine...the beginning spirits of the Rangers, the first 12].

The next step was a takeover of the entire alien ship.

Could 12 naked people do it? Each broke off a piece of pipe and fashioned a sharp weapon with it. Kull had no security or weapons onboard, because they felt in total control and had no need for weapons. It actually was a very easy matter for 12 strong, athletic types to wreak bloody vengeance against human/aliens that had decimated their planet.

These Rangers found material on the spaceship and made robes from the hempen cloth. They were as intelligent as they were in perfect, physical shape. *Was their boosted intelligence a lingered residue from being in a Union with a Snake?* In no time, the Kull language was deciphered and the 12 gained control of the ship.

They figured out how to operate the quantum-radio. They transmitted who they were and their location out to whomever listened. Why not? The crew had been damn lucky so far. Were there other lifeforms in space that might join them? Join them in their fight against the Kull? Suddenly...

They received a transmission! An answer to their message? OMG! It was from King Charles! The King of England? Apparently, it was. He told them: *"Sit tight, gang. We've monitored your situation and help is on the way! We have input coordinates to your ship's computer and it's on auto-pilot right now. We're taking you to our rebel base inside the Hollow Earth. Enjoy the ride to the South Pole, girls and boys. Charles out."*

[But the next scene showed that it was not King

Charles that sent a message to the group of rebels...It was Charlie!? And he was back to being a nasty Monitor!?? Black eyes, black tie, suit, sharp teeth, fangs and a fedora].

The crew maintained that it was truly the King. They were shocked, honored, overjoyed, overwhelmed and attempted a response with another radio transmission, but was unsuccessful. Hope. Faith. Fate. Maybe there were rebels against a tyrannical enemy and they were stronger than anyone imagined? A secret rebel base inside the planet? Maybe humanity would win, defeat the Kull in the end with secret weapons?

Jeff Janes led the crew who cheered and now believed there was a chance for a better life after the invasion. The ship reached Earth and zoomed toward the South Pole in its pre-programmed course. When it entered the frozen aperture of the Big Hole...*a sudden red ray from inside the Earth and from the largest Particle Beam Machine ever constructed, shattered the rebel ship to smithereens!!*

...When that happened, Charlie woke up! It was a dream. [?] After what had occurred on Earth in the Attack and the Purge, *the man* felt the need for sleep, to escape the Hell on Earth. He wanted to forget the horrors of the last few days. He learned to love the planet! He learned to love people! HE WAS A MAN. Not a Monitor. He no longer wanted to be alone; he wanted to be embraced, to be loved! But, now? Who was left? Just about no one. *Why was I spared?* "Why was I not touched in the annihilation, the Purge!?" he screamed at the top of his lungs. "Why?! To dream of rebels, rangers that will police the galaxy and make everything better?! Only to see them FAIL? To know that all hope is gone?!" Charles cried. He wasn't supposed to cry or have emotions, but he cried and he had too many emotions.

13. Aftermath

"Wake up!" Maxine yelled to her master. Or was it the other way around?

Charlie was jogged awake, shaken out of the second dream he'd ever had. The dream was a fabulous wonderland: a *PEZ Planet* where dispenser heads from the famous company lived and breathed. Things like the TACO and PIZZA-head were also there; *they were all there!* Excited to exist, excited to be alive! Chuck was so happy on PEZ Planet. He was safe. He wasn't alone and he had many friends in this special place. Charles hoped he'd return there in his next dream. If he stayed alive, that is? He continued to appear as a clean-shaven Carlito Alcaraz, only with long hair.

"You Okay?"

"Sure, sure. Where were you last night?" Charlie asked as he got up out of bed and walked toward the living room.

The white orb floated along and followed him. Maxine said, *"Hey, we're in a pickle here, a helluva situation! I checked out our options, not much we can do. Queen ain't answering. No one's coming to our rescue, boss..."*

"What's the danger here?"

"A second Purge is the danger, Charles. That could be at any time. I tried to gather information..."

"And you learned?"

"Ah, aw, hm...we have to go! And go now. Hey, do you know what will happen to me if you die?"

"No. What will happen?"

"I don't freaking know! And I'm a little scared, friend. I think I die too."

"Wait a minute, M. What are you talking about? I can't die. I'm an electric iso..." Charlie declared and thoroughly believed it at the moment.

"Ha, ha, ha! That's a good one. I needed a good laugh, pal. Do you know how long, how many seemingly centuries and transitions through dimensions, it's been since you were a Monitor? Where's your fangs and sharp teeth? That was lifetimes ago! You are, and I cannot account for this, a 100% human being now! Don't see how it's possible, but it's true."

"No, no, no. I still don't have to eat or piss..."

"That's because you remain a creature of Energy. If humans utilized more of their mind, as you do, people wouldn't have to eat or shit either. You're just more advanced and much farther along, evolutionary wise."

Charlie was amazed and also never feared for his life before. "But I could die??" The color on his face paled.

"Alright, gee whiz, I'll play Mother. Yes son, you are going to die, but it will be a very long time from now..."

"Yeah. Like today?" Worry was written across

Chuck's face. "Maybe I should go back to sleep, huh?"

"You know, Chief, we have nothing on the docket, no cases on our agenda...go ahead. Saw some lumber and have sweet dreams, my man."

"Sounds nice, lady. Afternoon delight. I'll see if I can program myself to reenter my last dream? Oh, the color, wow. The sweet smell. Music! I was having a good time and then I woke up on crappy, Silent Earth, hm. No fun."

"Goodnight, big guy. I'll see if I can tune in and watch the movie?"

"You do that, M. 'Night." Charlie walked back into his bedroom and threw himself on the bed. He got into his sleep-position on his right side. In minutes, he was asleep...

TS Caladan

14. Charles, King of PEZ Planet

It was magical. Is that simply a description of something that baffles Science? It was not long after Charlie's head hit the soft, white pillow that he reentered his PEZ Planet dream, exactly as he intended. His third dream. The man had more confidence now that he knew he was not just a mortal human being. He was a special kind of guy, someone highly evolved. He had forgotten...

His energy landed him in the bright, bright, colorful, colorful town of East McSweetport, with its main highways of Raspberry Street and Cherry Boulevard. *Yep, this was it!* He hardly remembered his first visit here. It was like a dream. But THIS! This was reality! So detailed, a visual splendor. And the exquisite air was intoxicating. Skies were beautifully turquoise-blue with a few billowy, white clouds. The buildings didn't appear like buildings that he was familiar with. They were modular, rounded structures, stacked on top of each other. Other buildings appeared as huge 'potatoes.' They towered high into the air and were crowned with what looked like antennae. He noticed a castle at the highest point, a small mountain in the distance. The town was fairly crowded, but no one was in his immediate area. Brightly colored vehicles sped along roads, only they were hovercrafts. No wheels. The 'cars' were rounded and rectangular. Of course, the hovercrafts were in the shape of PEZ tablets. Two-seaters, 4-seaters, 8-seaters, double-decker and triple-decker buses. There were also airships that flew in smooth/lovely arcs, high over buildings and were also rectangular in shape. Everything was intensely intricate and very colorful. The overall view resembled a Cartoon Land. Only Charlie did not appear CGI in any way. He was real.

What to do? Would the people and things know that I'm a virtual stranger here, an alien? I am not a PEZ dispenser. I wonder if they'll know? "I know. I'll hail a cab and that should be a nice tour where I can ask questions. Cabbies like to talk. Ah, there's one now! Speak of the..." Charlie waved his human hand and a brilliant red-orange taxi pulled over.

The driver smiled and was a type of sea creature (Sebastian from 'Little Mermaid'). "Need a lift?" the friendly red/orange crab asked.

"Indeed I do, friend."

"Hop in. Where ya going? I sure haven't seen you before."

"I am a stranger, just got here."

"Ah, new model, eh?" Sebastian commented. He hit the lever and the meter clicked on and timed the ride.

"Uh...*yeah.* I need a guide. To show me around McSweetport, you know? Are there, ah, hot spots, you know, cool sites we could check out?"

"Cool sites, you say? I saw some cool sites when I was in Paris..."

"Yeah?"

"Yeah, they were parasites. Ugh, *awful critters.* Ah, ha, ha, ha," Sebastian was proud of himself.

"Very funny. I'll remember that. *Hey, keep your eyes on the road, eh?* I don't want to die in my dream..."

"Oh, no one dies here, sir. It's one big/happy party all the time. Oh jeez, I am runnin' low on fuel. You mind terribly if we stop at a station, sir?"

"Please. And call me Charlie."

"Charlie, I like that. Call me: Seb, for Sebastian," the crab said. They came upon a refueling station in less than a minute and the driver pulled in.

Chuck lowered his edible glass window, not before he licked it. He got a better look at the place. He wanted to see everything, every movement, everything these sweet people and things did.

The cab idled in the air and the crab got out. He waddled to the green and orange pumps and approached a little hole that was near the bottom of one particular pump [high octane]. Sebastian tossed in three PEZ pellets into the hole, one at a time. Suddenly, the pump pulsated and was ready to shoot fuel out of the hose. He was able to get the hose into the port on the bottom of the cab before the fuel rushed out.

Charlie watched the little guy with fascination. Soon, Seb was back in the driver's seat, on top of the pillow and smiled big.

"Let me ask you, what's this fuel you're putting into the vehicle, Seb?"

"Oh. It's a...(fished through his pocket)...*this*. Well, a liquefied version of it." The crab held up an orange PEZ candy tablet. He tossed it in his mouth. "Mm, PEZ petrol."

"Huh. That fuels everything, I imagine? Amazing."

"Yes, sir. Even us." Open the little drawer on the back of my seat," Seb suggested. The drawer was filled with Orange PEZ. "Help yourself. My favorite's orange. Don't you like orange the best?"

Charlie wasn't about to argue. He was happy and grabbed a handful of Orange and casually consumed them. "Good."

"I know where I want to take you first. We're really proud of this place in our wonderful town. It's very famous. We have tourists from other areas drive through it every day. It is a high-population place; it's where most of us live...in the Labyrinth."

"Labyrinth?" Charlie was curious. He looked upward as if it *struck a bell.*

"There's the top of the structure now. See it?" The crab pointed a big claw.

"That's a labyrinth?"

"It will be minutes before we get there. Hmm. What else? Oh, we have a geyser that blows at the same time everyday. The young ones love it."

"Hang on, Seb. Day? You mean, you have night here? Everything's so bright and colorful and the darkness of night is coming? I didn't see a sun..."

"Ha, ha, no sir. There's no night in the Dream World, nothing dark or negative at all here, Charlie. That was just an expression..."

"Then you know this is a dream?"

"Of course. We all do. Ha. Nothing like this could ever be real, eh?"

Chuck remembered the high castle and asked, "I guess you have a King? I saw the castle on the hill..."

"Oh, that is one sad thing for our whole PEZ Planet. We have no King. A King was supposed to appear by now according to prophecy, but the inhabitants of this world have waited and waited and there's been no sign of a King, anywhere..."

"Well, what's this King supposed to look like? How would you know it if he suddenly appeared?"

Seb replied, "The old books describe him with a special *mark* and as a person different than any other. He is a good-looking man with long, brown hair..."

"I have long, brown hair," Chuck told the crab.

Sebastian turned around and got a better look into the backseat. "So you do. Ha! That be funny, if I was driving around the Man Who Would Be King. HAA! Oh, by the way, we do have a Queen..."

"Oh, you do. What's she like?"

"Sad," Seb admitted. "More sadness, in our world

that doesn't really have sadness. She has no King, Charlie. She's alone and waits and waits, ah...sad."

Chuck asked: "Is she pretty?"

"We've never seen her. We're told about her from her guards. She's supposed to be a raving beauty. Never made a public appearance. But of course, if a King showed up, I'm sure they'd appear on the royal balcony and greet throngs of happy, happy subjects. Ah, kinda takes your breath away, eh?"

"I'd like to meet her," he said innocently.

"Ha, ha, ha! Good luck with that, Chuck."

"Hey. That Labyrinth is big. Look at it..."

"Ha, yeah, I've seen it. Here we go, the main drag." Sebastian turned the PEZ mobile over an 8-lane highway, the start of the Maze. The wide road diverged into numerous single avenues, and then to many ways to go, while very high walls were on either side of roadways. The massive walls were wooden and the townies lived in dwellings, condos, apartments, compartments, floor after floor, high into the sky! People and things were seen on overhang balconies. Some had parties, but mostly the wooden balconies were empty. People and things were off doing other activities.

"I like to dream, Charlie," Seb said out of the blue.

"Me too."

"...Just imagine if a King really showed up and had ME, little ol' me, drive the Royal Carriage that held King and Queen. Wow. And if *that* happened and we drove through the Labyrinth, every single person and thing would be out on their balconies, looking through windows, cheering, shouting, playing music, tossing confetti! Oh, God. That would be something to see, eh?" Seb said with wide eyes.

"It's a good dream, Seb. Good luck with that too," Charlie said sincerely.

"Oh, there's someone I know. Let me pull over and say *hi?*"

"Fine," Charlie said.

The cab parked on the side of the road next to a raccoon.

Sebastian shouted out of his window: "I didn't expect to see you here, *a Guardian!* Hiya doin', old friend? This is Charlie, a new guy. I'm touring him around. *Say, Rocket,* is there trouble?"

"I'm bored, is what it is. There's *never* any trouble around here!" Rocket said loudly with his furry arms raised. "Hi, guy. Seb, your passenger looks weird. Then I guess we all look a bit strange now, huh? Ha, ha."

"How are the other Guardians?" Sebastian asked his buddy.

"Starlord is very bored with nothing to do so he's teaching us how to play baseball, of all things. Can you imagine the Guardians as a baseball team? Ha."

Seb replied: "You got the big guy. He'd be good..."

"You know what we need? I hate to say it, but we need some trouble, a crisis, some small disaster. You know, so the good guys can swoop in and save the day, eh?"

"Can I ask you a question?" Charlie said from the backseat window.

The raccoon replied: "You just did." Then he *blasted off!* Rocket's rockets fired and they propelled him high into the air and he took off in another direction.

"Isn't he a funny guy? Ha, ha. Ah. Oh, what was your question, Charlie?"

"Well, he seemed like an official with that ray-gun or maybe one of the Queen's guards? I was going to ask: Could he get me an audience with the Queen?"

"Ha! You have spunk, son. I like that. I'm gonna drive you to the Royal Castle right now and I've never taken anyone there before..."

"You will?!" Charles was extremely excited. He thought: *Why do I feel this is fate?* [He accessed: movies]. *I'm different. I know she'll see me just like I got in to see the PEZ President. I just know it!*

Sebastian started up the hovercraft and the car moved quickly over one of the avenues that led out of the Labyrinth.

Seb said, "People should get their dreams, good dreams, you know? Everyone should receive exactly what they deserve. Hey, friend, when yer rubbin' elbows with the Queen, don't forget to mention *me*, the guy who helped you out and tell her, ah..."

"What?"

"...Tell her I'm the best driver in town, for goodness sake! It's true. If she ever does make a public appearance, I'm her crab."

"Ha, ha. You got it, bud. Ha, I just realized: yer a crabbie, a crabby cabbie."

"Funny. Ha, ha. That's good." They laughed and made more small talk as they rode up the inclined road called 'Haas Highway.' They were minutes away from the front guards and the colorful castle's moat.

"I know why I appear different from all of you here. I have a surprise for you, Seb. Something I need to show you," the man stated in a serious tone. "Maybe you should pull over, before you see it? You're a dream-weaver too, and your dreams will come true..."

"Wow. Mysterious." The crab stopped the motion of the hovercraft. (Maybe the little guy felt it also?). Seb turned completely around with big, curious eyes.

"What do you think of this, my friend?" The man revealed a birthmark on his chest. It could be read as: '*pez.*'

The sea creature got brighter and brighter and his whole face lit up. He stammered, stuttered and out came: "Y-y-your, your Ma, Ma, Majesty." He bowed.

"No Sebastian, don't do that. Later, I'll introduce you to the Queen..."

Later...

They got in! The mark. The birthmark was all that it

took to get through the guards (Superman, Wonder Woman and Batman), traverse the moat bridge, raise the giant front gate and have an immediate audience with the Queen.

"Aaaaaaaah," Charlie breathed a big sigh of relief. "I was worried, Seb. But now I know that everything's gonna be alright. Looks like I'm getting my Dream. Ah." Then a broader smile formed on his face. They were inside the stunning and incredibly ornate walls of Castle PEZ. Boba Fett, the Mandalorian and six white Stormtroopers had escorted the man and his driver into the heart of the castle, just short of the grand doors before her throne room.

Sebastian shook and stood at the foot of the man. He expressed, "I can't believe I'm here with you. I'm nervous and s-scared, Charlie. I think she eats crab..."

"C'mon, man. Nothing bad happens on this planet. You said so..."

"Oh yeah, goodness me. Why would I ever think such a thing?"

The huge doors with PEZ sigils on them opened with a loud "creeeeeck" and trumpets blared! The man and the crab walked in as soon as they could. Seb trailed behind. Background music lowered its volume and there was a suspenseful silence.

Her jeweled, golden throne was spectacular and lay ahead of them. The Queen was nowhere to be seen at the moment. Along the walls were a line of Stormtroopers, plus the Justice League, Thor, Spiderman, Ironman, Dr. Strange, the Avengers, the Hulk, X-Men, male Captain Marvel, female Captain Marvel and the Guardians.

The duo inched closer and closer to the throne. Rocket couldn't believe his eyes that Seb waddled in right behind the guy in the backseat. He wanted to react but was under strict protocols to not move until commanded to. Seb smiled and waved~.

Charles wanted to make a strong, dramatic entrance so he removed his shirt. He displayed the unique birthmark and the whole court saw how different he was.

GASPS and loud murmurs from the superheroes echoed throughout the great throne room once the royal guards observed the special image on his bare chest.

Here was the KING. Where was the Queen? Charles felt she would also make a dramatic entrance on the scene from behind the sheer curtains right in back of the throne. Then an unusual thought struck him. He looked down at his orange/red friend and asked, "Psssst. Seb. I'm about to meet the Queen. What do I call her outside of 'Your Majesty' and 'Your Grace.' What's her name?"

"Ah, her name? Why, it's...Queen Catwallender..."

"Wot?!" He was going to fall to his knees anyway, but, when he heard her name, his knees buckled, his body turned to goo and he crashed onto the royal floor...

This was perfectly timed with her bloody entrance as she thrust through the light curtains and shouted for all to hear: "My KING! Long live the King!"

It was fur-head Catwallender who was now a full feline and had a fur-body, sharp claws and a long tail.

Charles fainted dead away...

Later...

When Charlie came to his senses, another strange scene surrounded him...

They had brought in a King's Throne and he was upon it, only he was dressed in the King's royal attire: a violet uniform, trimmed in white. Medals on his chest. Someone dressed him. He wore a jeweled crown and held a scepter in his right-hand. They were alone. No guards. And SHE sat next to him on the Queen's throne.

"Hi. Fancy seeing you here," she said to him.

"Me? Hold on one cotton-pickin' minute! This is a beautiful dream world of mine so why in Ann Arbor would YOU be the Queen?!"

"Why not, big boy?"

"Oh yeah, you were the one who changed them all to your *cute* image. Every last one of them and put a spell on everybody, yes? I mean in the real world?"

Catwallender said: *"I didn't come to play. I came to play. This is your dream. It's not on me, it's on you, Booboo. Remember your EFFECT on the world, eh?"*

"So what's going to happen here now? It's a little creepy with you here, you know? You don't really fit in. I might just want to wake up and join the real world?"

"And miss all the fun I plan?" She roared a laugh,

"HA! Wait 'til you see!"

"What?" Charles dreamed of a PEZ Paradise. But paradises never last, do they? His fears might not be controlled here? His fears might be manifested here?

The Queen answered the King with one word to sum it up: ***"Darkness."***

He gasped.

"Please remember, Charles: This was your fault. You changed everything here when you first arrived. C'mon. You've planted evil seeds before. Remember? You've been the Destroyer of Worlds before, Chucky. Remember 'I am become'?"

Maybe I did do this? He freaked. *But I'm completely different now!* A new thought struck him and he asked, "Where's Sebastian? Where's my driver?"

She stared at Chuck with large cat eyes and said, *"His legs were delicious."*

"Ah." The man nearly fainted and almost puked in disgust.

Queen Catwallender laughed hysterically and then got her furry ass off the throne and walked in one particular direction. *"Come with me, lover boy. You can leave the crown and scepter. I want to show you more of what you've done to Paradise. This was your fault."* She turned her back and walked toward an archway.

Charlie tossed the crown and scepter aside and followed her.

They reached the Cat's personal boudoir, the royal

bedroom. There was a lot of cat hair everywhere. There were two large shutters that sealed every bit of outside sights and sounds. They were high up and would have a fantastic view of her domain if the shutters were opened. She casually strolled over to the shutters and opened them...

"Aaaaaah!!" Charles screamed.

It was pitch black over her empire. **NIGHT**. Miles away, and Charles heard screams from the townies. His sweet dream turned into a horrible nightmare.

After a frozen moment of terror, he pushed out of his mouth the words: "Cats are supposed to be...*good*. They, they...they take away everything...bad..." The man said slowly. He was supremely dazed and wished he could switch himself (energy, spirit) to a different place. He dreamed that he could wake up...

She replied; *"That's in the real world, honey. Where do you think you are? And, dear boy, who says I'm a cat? How about a couple more surprises, Charlie? I wonder if your two hearts can take it? Huh?"*

"What are you talking about?" The man felt there was a tsunami-worth of truth that he was unaware of and soon he'd be splashed with the full force of a titanic Wave...

"Since all the cards are on the table and all the chips tossed into the center, the truth is: There was never a Maxine. Or I should say, she's ME! You idiot! How did you, you higher evolved person, not know that?? But

that's not half of it, ha, ha, ha. **I'm your bloody Queen, you worm, you scum, you bug, you MAN! Remember ME?!"**

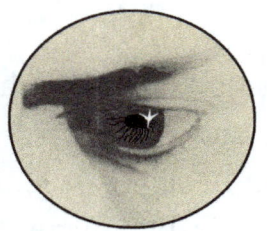

When her logo appeared, Charlie felt like the biggest fool, ever! *Yeah, I shudda known.* "Queen ZEP. Queen Zep, all this time?" he said to himself. *Yeah.* He felt sick and stupid. Actually he wanted to die, but he couldn't. *Why? Why?* The man asked her, directly: "Why did you do this?! Why did you fuck up a lovely dream?"

Catwallender/Maxine or just plain ol' ZEP, answered: **"I don't know. I simply sense joy in watching you suffer, aye? I think I've been rather consistent this whole time, my son."**

More screams were heard outside the high window.

Chuck closed the shutters. He was very sad and very confused. (Sometimes, sometimes when things were at their worst...*it changed*). He kept hope alive in his hearts. Suddenly, he had a *revelation* as if a bolt of golden lightning struck his brain. *Maybe it's true if I believe it's true?* He knew something that Queen ZEP did not.

<>With the idea accepted and believed in his soul, Charles became (in a sense) a good and true KING. He could do anything. He was over the Queen, but not over

the Ace. Charles, now Saint Charles, desired to WAKE...and he did. *He woke up.*

Charlie was inside his cottage home that he bought with the Multi-Pass and was seated up on his bathroom sink, a bathroom that he never used. He woke from sleep leaned up against the sizable mirror. "Uh." But he wasn't old Charlie anymore. He was clean. He was clear. He didn't have one drop of negativity in his flesh, blood and bones. This one was never a Monitor, never was bald, never had fangs and sharp teeth, never liked suits and ties and absolutely hated fedoras! The man never had roots in evil and never did bad deeds in the past. His name was not Charles. Not anymore.

His head turned and he looked at the man in the mirror. THERE HE WAS! *That* was the demon-Charles, with his Black Effect on everything he touched. There was the one who changed utopia into hell and light into dark. *He's the one with the devilish connections, not me!*

The reflection in the mirror was not a devil. It merely cast a reverse image.

The man understood that he was in the real world now and the entire panoramic scope of witchcraft, fascism, hatred, horror, blood and guts and downright dark evilness will not now or later ever dominate the physical world. Thanks to this man [unknown galactic hero at the moment], oceans/volumes and tons of

Negativity have been trapped, locked away forever in his dream world. That's where all the hate and anti-love was poured into. And that Nightmare and all of its heavy dark-matter weight...*went up in a puff of smoke,* as soon as he awoke. Today, it was a brighter Danos Galaxy. Prettier.

TS Caladan

15. Rebel Lodges

This particular lodge had a number like every lodge had a number. Lodges were named by local agents who used them. This one was: 'Light Hawk' and was considered the best, the prime meeting establishment for the newly formed (secret) Rangers. The Solar System finally had a police force, a 'Wings Over the World,' also referred to as the 'Justice League.' Sort of. And it was about time that somebody with a little power and clout cleaned up renegade, out-of-control planets. Tried to. Tyrants have taken over many worlds. Royals, tin-gods, generals, majors, lifeforms drunk with power, and they ruled. Whomever possessed the Power on planets, moons, space stations: They set the laws. Terrible/terrible atrocities, mass-murders, wars, genocide, have occurred all because of the *fucking, fucking, fucking, fucking Prime Directive!*

"Screw the Prime Directive!!" was heard again and again, recently, over Media and Mega Media and within new guilds and lodges.

There was an understanding as part of an ancient treaty set up by the Lizards long ago, who filed valid claims on planets in this section of Danos and in other galaxies. Reptilian species would never overtly (militaristically) force their empire upon the surfaces of these planets that they OWNED. No. They operated covertly, behind the scenes, and did their own 'thing,' invisibly or unknown to those who believed they ruled the planet. *The Lizards allowed anyone to do anything* [not particle beams shot at stars or planets]. Whomever migrated to whatever planet and established their reign, could control it any way they saw fit. Rule of the jungle: the strongest survived. Big, cold, 2-legged Reptiles let everyone alone and stayed out of the way. They established the 'Prime Directive' out of many directives and that was:

No one can invade these planets and change anything. It was the Law. The big, dark-green Lizards were nasty, but they were fair. They have stepped in and settled disputes between tribes of nations (planets), but these cases were rare and would have resulted in the destruction of the planet. The Lizards do not care about humans, aliens or any lifeforms that occupy their planets. They were much more worried about the property than the people [like landlords].

The result is a horrific situation in the galaxy. What human being or any compassionate lifeform can stand by and do nothing when others suffer? *Humans and aliens cannot help other humans and aliens.* Each world was sovereign. Outsiders (invaders) cannot alter what the leaders of that particular planet have instituted. No matter how cruel, how heartless or how against LIFE it was.

There were planets of abundance that could distribute "care-packages" of food to the poor and needy. There was technology, Tesla's wireless principles of Free Energy that could be shared with world after world! Antigravity! *Miracles could happen,* if they were only allowed.

They're not. Not in the Danos Galaxy and not in other galaxies where cold-blooded Reptilians owned planets.

Over time, the situation had caused a reverse-ripple effect. In other words: REBELLION, hence the Rebel Lodges: A galactic underground, hush-hush, spy-stuff, where radicals against the Empire or any injustice met, organized, reported news and got stinking drunk. They were far from an elite fighting force or real Policemen. This was the beginning of the Rangers. They had hit planets hard with food, supplies, data, technology and even arms, but weapons that were always placed in good hands.

<>One evening, a strange man walked into the Light Hawk and sat down on a comfy seat at a table in the corner, alone. His name was Mister Carpenter. He was a strong, fit, young man, clean-shaven with long, brown hair. He ordered blue Mead from the attractive waitress. He caught the attention of local agents. Mister Carpenter was a telepath and knew that his coming here would interest the secret Rangers. He was curious. *Wonder what will happen in the lodge I've heard so much about?*

Here they come, he thought.

Three of them, strapping lads in colorful garb, skulked over to his table and made sure they plastered smiles on their dirty faces. Carpenter's mind gave them the names: 'Porky,' 'Too Tall' and 'Stupid.'

The tall one spoke first: "'Aven't seen you 'ere before, stranger..."

Porky backed him up with: "You don't mind if we join you, eh mate?"

Carpenter happily replied, "Not at all! I was looking for company, lads." He turned to the waitress and shouted to everyone: "Drinks for everyone! The lot of you! On me!"

More than a dozen men cheered the newcomer! "Yay!" "That's what I'm talking about!" "Jolly good." "Double-Plus!" "Why don't you ever pick up the tab?"

Did the ploy work? Mister Carpenter thought: *Maybe these men won't kill me now? Ha.* Four glasses of Mead (blue and green) were brought to his table. Each sat around the round table as if they were the best of friends. He went with his feelings and asked them, "I have a few questions for you blokes I'd like to know, eh?"

Porky, Too Tall and Stupid laughed out loud. "Ha, ha, haaaaa!" Stupid stated, "That's awfully fantastical 'cos we got some questions for *you,* ha!" They all laughed. Stupid continued his train of thought: "Sees, we dun know if yer one of those *Rangers* on the news, we been hearin' about....or...or..." (Stupid dazed off for seconds).

Too Tall took over the talk: "...Or, or, 'e's trying to say, or, are you a Ranger-Hunter? Eh? *Ranger-Hunter?!* Seeking out rebels? Killin' 'em for the Galactic State?! Here in the best lodge? Guess you think this is our secret headquarters, aye?"

The other two poor excuses for 'Rebel Rangers' knew that Too Tall made a major mistake with his emotional words. Shouldn't have hinted that this was *their* rebel base. The two others waved their heads back and forth and made weird faces.

This cracked up Carpenter and he shouted with laughter: "Haw! Haaaa, ha, eh, oh my. That's too funny." The outburst got the attention of the crowd. "Here's what's funny..." He pointed at Stupid. "Even the dumb one knew that was wrong, ha, ha, ha!"

The three got to their feet and stood over the man. Porky was pissed and wanted to fight. They each wanted to fight and Mister Carpenter knew that from the beginning. The chubby one declared, "You know, boys, I suddenly don't like da looks on this character. He should come down a peg...even though he bought drinks."

No one in the crowd intervened. Some of them wanted to see action and witness a fight. Riots, brawls often happened in guilds and lodges where rowdy boys got drunk, got high and wanted to prove what a *man* they were to other men.

Carpenter smiled and remained seated. He

understood them. *They just want to flex their muscles, intimidate and see if they can get away with it. I like spunk.*

Three Rangers grabbed him at the same time, just to see what he would do!

He pushed a button on a weapon they didn't know was hooked to his belt and A POWERFUL, BLUE, PHOTONIC SHAFT OF ELECTRIC ENERGY about 5 feet long SMASHED upward, through the wooden table and shattered it to pieces!! *BAM! Vvvvuuummm.* The drinks flew. The Light-Sword was swung inches away from Too Tall's head. Everyone was fine and everyone was completely shocked. No one had ever seen a light-weapon like that before.

It took a minute for everything and everybody in the Light Hawk Lodge to settle down. The three Rangers were motionless, like frozen statues. Background music played once more.

The man with the blue light-weapon pressed the button again and the photonic energy of the Light-Sword disappeared with a *Vvvvuuummm.* Mister Carpenter stood tall and saw the proprietor who had not said a word. He reached into his pocket and pulled out a rod of pure pink tourmaline, very clear, very valuable, about 4 inches long and tossed it to the proprietor. "For the damage I caused, sir. That should make amends; won't happen again, I assure you...ah, also, another round of drinks!"

"Yeeeees!" was collectively yelled by the happy

patrons [drinks and a show].

The proprietor had them bring in a new table and some of the mess was cleaned up. The three Rangers slowly sat down and joined Mister Carpenter, a little different than it was in the beginning. They saw new blue and green Meads were on the table. The waitress winked at Mister Carpenter. Everything was back to normal.

The 3 ragtag, unorganized and shaken Rangers traded stares between them. There were smiles throughout the lodge. Mister Carpenter smiled also and knew the dumb one (who he liked) would speak first and say something funny.

Stupid came to the massive conclusion: "Hey, men...I fink we can use this fellow."

Porky piggybacked a question: "Would you like to be a Ranger, sir?"

Mister Carpenter only laughed loud and then stayed silent...

The stunning events of the evening were far from over. The patrons will soon have much more to talk about and tell their children for years to come all because of things to come this night at Light Hawk Lodge...

Next, THE DEVIL WALKED IN THE DOOR!

TS Caladan

16. The Devil vs. PEZ

He was a very deep red humanoid, strong arms, strong legs, a frightening face, long horns, fangs, claws and a long tail. He stood 7-foot tall and was naked. Sixteen patrons of the well-known lodge backed away from the bloody monster as soon as it entered. Carpenter, the agents and the rest of the humans could not take their eyes off the creature. Was this really the Devil, as portrayed in films and illustrated in artwork down through the ages? Who was the scary red brute that appeared as if it could crush boulders and eat people whole?

Rangers slowly moved to where they could get their hands on blaster weapons and were at the ready. Of course, there was Mister Carpenter who'd more than likely join the battle, if there was another fight in the lodge?

The 'Devil' gruffed and huffed and grabbed the largest wooden chair and slid it to the center of the room. He sat as if he was exhausted and had just experienced some emotional/inner trauma to his 'black soul.' His loud voice said the words:

"Gosh, jeez Louise, have you ever been married, fellows? Got some advice for you dudes: Don't ever marry a *woman!* Can you relate, boys? They're awful! They tease you, they seduce you, they love you, they worship you...and, and, the next day, *they rip your nuts off!* Man, do I need a drink!"

Less than a half minute later, Rangers piled a few goblets of green Mead on the floor around him, within his reach and then they moved away.

"Thanks, boys. Don't worry, I'll pay for these." The *Devil* drank. "Aww, that's good! Yeah."

The crowd listened intently to the guy with scarlet skin when he continued:

"...And *she's on the phone now!* Torturing me. She yells at me and makes me feel like I can do nothing right! Everything I do is *wrong!* FUCK! Ah, you know what I mean? This is maddening! She orders me around...and, and, fuck I do it! Why do I obey her every whim? She thinks she's a Queen! See, I'm just feedin' into her power trip and control. I give 'r 'r way, why do I do that!??" The creature had finished the first goblet and worked on the second. "Aaaaaaaah, right." He breathed deep, burped and only now moved his horned head around to see what was in the big room.

It just so happened that *Lucifer* sat right across from Mister Carpenter's chair. They looked directly into each other's eyes. And smiled. They almost bowed and did not know why.

The Devil said to everyone, while his eyes were locked directly onto the man with long, brown hair:

"How does she know everything? Tell me, how does that happen? For example, she says I'll meet a mysterious man from China, an old sage wizard named Lin Wu, and..."

Some of the crowd had heard of Lin Wu and repeated the name. A few expressed awe as if the Chinese man was supremely holy and very powerful. There were gasps, murmurs, whispers and chatter...

"...Oh, you know the guy?" The satanic creature expressed after he heard the crowd's response. He continued with a story: "...Let me tell you what happened. I run into this character in a crowded alley in Zagreb and he begs me for money. I didn't know he was Lin Wu, ancient wizard with magical powers. *So I smash his face!* Big mistake. Boy, I sure should have tossed him a few sheckles. Next thing I know, I'm lifted high into the air. *'E was doing it with his mind, 'e was!* I'm waving back and forth high in the air! Then...then, I'm thrust toward a brick wall and the son-of-a-bitch makes me STOP an inch before I hit. I shit right there, man..."

Some of the crowd laughed. *Maybe this guy was alright?*

"...Oh, ah. So, so, instead of him flattening me like a pancake, 'e puts this Spell on me and now I look like this, aye?" Look at ME!!" The creature grabbed his thick, anaconda-like tail and twirled it in the air! His once horrific face was now a sympathetic/silly face that displayed sad aggravation and frustration.

More laughter was heard around the red demon.

Mister Carpenter laughed and spoke up and asked, "You're not the Devil?"

"Didn't you hear my story, sir? I'm Asir Benwobbe, goat-herder. And I'm married to a real bitch! I think *she's* responsible, now that I come to think of it." He rubbed his black claws against his chin. *"She* told me where to go, that alley. You see, my wife's a true Mystic, *you don't know!* Psychic. Bet she set me up and knew this would happen, even WANTED this to happen! Huh. She calls *me* the Devil, but it's her, it's her, *she's the Devil!* Fucking Queen of the Black Arts bitch! I swear it's like she controls the world. *She channels!* Yeah! She channels this, this, ah, Queen character. What's her name? Aaaah..."

"Ha, ha, sorry friend," Mister Carpenter said aloud and admitted, "I don't mean to make light of your dire situation, Mister Benwobbe. That's one helluva Spell yer under. I'd hate to be seen as the Devil. You say, your lovely wife's on the phone?"

"Here, *you* talk to her." Asir threw the phone out of his chest as if from nowhere. It was a reflex action and he didn't know why he did it, but he did...

Carpenter caught the device and understood that this man was fully clothed. He was a goat-herder who used a cell phone. The horned-devil image was only a layer, a coating or a skin placed overtop his actual appearance. The man with the light-sword whose face resembled

Carlito Alcaraz and had long, brown hair...pushed a button on Mister Benwobbe's phone. He was as casual as a cucumber and knew what he was doing. He knew who was on the phone with him and it was not this man's wife...

Oh, no. It was the THING, "entity," monster that spoke through her on the phone. The small audience was hypnotized, unclear what it was they witnessed.

Carpenter was cool. "Hello, Queen ZEP! How are you, dear girl? Wait, I don't care. Must speak the truth, you know? That's my own personal curse, eh?" He nodded to Mister Benwobbe. "...Are you there, my former Queen?"

"You bastard! How did this happen? How the HEAVEN did so much EVIL disappear from that galaxy? Okay, it was fun to fuck with Asir. But this is actually about you, son. You were supposed to really, really, really screw up Danos, eh? Plant your evil seeds that spread like cancer and here make worlds living hells!! THAT DIDN'T HAPPEN!! I can't explain it! Look at you, what a failure in my eyes. You look like a good, handsome, all-powerful Superhero! You were supposed to turn into a Beast! Beast-Mode. A Killer! Not a beautiful human being with feelings and compassion! Augh! What happened? Can you explain it to me, son?"

Carpenter smiled and looked around at the confused and twisted faces in the crowd. He calmly replied, "Sure.

Sure. My Lady. I can explain it. Thought you knew?"

"Well? What?!"

He made the Queen wait. "Ha, ha...this is fun. Better than exploring. Okay, I'll tell you. Ha, ha. Man, are you going to laugh. I ate the PEZ..."

"Wot?"

"I ate the PEZ. Mmm."

"You weren't supposed to eat the PEZ. I especially and specifically insisted that you do not eat the bleeding PEZ now, didn't I?!"

"I wanted to try it, mum. Ha, ha."

"All the reports said you did not eat it. Everything, my whole PLAN in Danos was based on you NOT eating the PEZ! Maxine told me you didn't. That freaking, lying BITCH!! Ugh....Did you really eat it?"

"I ate it. Huh. Thought she was you?"

"Augh!"

The female creature, whatever it was, on the other end of the phone, simply collapsed and cried. It was an embarrassing scene for the "Holy Sovereign."

[click].

Mister Carpenter immediately crushed the phone in his hand and lined up a toss that was more than 40-feet to a trashcan and flung it...right in! The gang cheered at the goal and also cheered at: "Another round of drinks!"

Loud music played. There was excitement in the air and drinks were drunk in the prime lodge. People were joyous. They were going to start dancing. But, they saw the "Devil" in the middle of the room and changed their minds. Amir was hard to ignore. He remained a seated, 7-foot devil. His hand on his chin held a sorrowful face, while one bare foot tapped to the music. What would happen to Mister Benwobbe?

Then. In walked another character essential to the strange events of the night: Lin Wu. He was recognized and most of the crowd reacted to his presence with whispers. *The venerated Holy Man was actually in the Light Hawk.* He was tall, very thin and had to have been 200 years old. His face healed. The music stopped again.

When Amir saw the wizard, he yelled, "That's the *guy!* He's the one, the one who did this to me!"

"...And have come to undo, my brother. You have enough suffered." Lin Wu placed a frail, old hand on Amir's shoulder and the Spell was broken. The Devil 'clothing' was gone.

"Oh, thank you, thank you, Master Wu!" Mister Benwobbe cried in pure bliss. "OH! Here, sir. Please. I have money for you..."

Lin Wu waved a weak hand for *no.*

Amir should not have asked, but he did: "Is there anything you could do about my wife, great Master?"

The wise man shook his head slightly for *no.* He was about to laugh and placed his hand over his mouth. Then Lin Wu laughed a little.

"Oh well. I tried." The goat-herder was thrilled to

not appear as Satan anymore and *ran out of the place.*

Lin Wu turned to Carpenter who got to his feet and faced him. "You..."

"Me..."

"Also you enough suffered. Here for you...Heart Center..."

"What? What did you call me?"

Lin Wu approached and touched him on the shoulders. He said, "Your new name. You are Heart Center, leader of the Rangers."

This stunned the crowd, especially the agents that heard.

The wizard pulled on the man's shirt and revealed his *Kingly Birthmark.* This again shocked the crowd and confirmed everything: The Carpenter was the true King!

Instead of accepting the task, the responsibility, he questioned it: "These fools? You want me to lead them? They're idiots!"

"Hey, hey, we heard that." A lot of *rustling* among the insulted patrons.

"Yes..." Lin Wu agreed. "Rough. Need training. Or? Or save time...ahead jump?"

"What?"

The Chinese sage said: "Magicians know...no magic exists. All is Trick. I am...no Magician." The wizard waved a thin arm, and...

Reality changed. The covert rebel leaders were not a ragtag team of undisciplined, untrained, soldiers secretly against injustice anymore. <u>Future was now</u>. Suddenly, they were a polished, organized troop of neatly dressed (dark blue robed) revolutionaries with high-tech equipment and weapons. They all had light-swords. Rangers no longer hid. Rebels were not underground anymore; they were out in the open and dominated. They were powerful, they were a true 'Justice League.' They were the Police. [The Lizards were pissed, but were gone]. Rangers had spaceships, monitored situations via the ZEDNAR and had access to Star Gates, Time Machines and Minority Reports! *It happened in a blink of an eye.* The same characters were inside the Light Hawk, only a time-jump gave it a very different *skin* or upgrade.

Patrons did not react to the transition. To them, there was no change of reality. Time simply moved forward<.

In the recent past, Rangers had successfully created peace, order and far better conditions in many star systems. *There was no more Prime Directive because everyone decided to do the right thing and* **Break The Prime Directive!** Humans and aliens aided other humans and aliens on other worlds. Food, technology, energy, power sources and fantastic knowledge went where they were needed. Positive changes were mandated and improved over time. There were no more Wars between Worlds. Danos was a shining example of a galaxy that functioned well, in peace and harmony, with a good sense of Community and where people and aliens cared.

{Did this all happen because of PEZ Candy?}

Lin Wu's new assignment for the Rangers:

They must travel back in time and to another galaxy, to their "Twin Sister" galaxy of Darkmoor, but so long ago that it was known as the Milky Way. The wizard, and a Quantum Matrix Engine, would make that possible on a journey (in suspended animation) to the next galaxy. Time would be *reversed,* move in the other direction, for every lightyear the ship sped away from Danos. The voyage would be precisely timed so that when they got to their destination, it would be the perfect time that Time Machines showed for the origin of the Rangers in another galaxy.

Before Lin Wu *departed* the Light Hawk Lodge that unusual evening, he had more words for his seasoned, polished soldiers in the fight for Truth, Justice and Love of Life. He stared at the young Heart Center and smiled. Lin Wu understood that his wizard powers, or traces of his great abilities, were not wasted on this man. He was a strong leader and did tremendous things for the Light forces in Danos. He and his Rangers were needed elsewhere, tomorrow. They had to go. They were FATED to go, according to Time Windows and Time Machines. They had to save another galaxy, go back and plant their own sweet seeds of positive life and Complete a Great Circle...

Lin Wu sat down and was physically very tired after the enormous mental exertion where he *fixed worlds* and made sure timelines stayed secure without chaotic ripples that disturbed the perfection of what Must Be. He was pleased with the fact that *he'd soon be dead>*. Heart Center and the Brave (Porky), the Honest (Too Tall) and the Innocent (Stupid) also sat. The old man generated enough energy and explained the details of the next assignment in the Milky Way...

But Lin Wu had to laugh. (cough, cough) "Heart. Ha. Heart. (cough) Your job, very large, much/much bigger than suspect. Rangers will succeed...there. But. But. Problem (cough)..."

"Always a problem, eh? No stability, always a change?" Heart Center asked from his hearts.

"Ha...ah, yes. Problem *big* 'cos when arrive..." The wizard lost consciousness for a few seconds.

"Great Master?"

"...Here. Unless Lin Tao walk in. Ha."

The Innocent whispered to Heart Center, "Who's Lin Tao?"

HC replied, *"His* Master." Heart smiled, turned to Lin Wu and stated: "Yer still cracking jokes, Master?"

He breathed heavily and answered, "Did I tell you...importance...laughter?"

"Yes." Heart smiled again with tears in his eyes. He asked, "What big problem? Lin?"

He responded with these words: "When arrive...Rangers be, be..."

"What?"

"...Very, very...small."

Heart Center searched his senses and got a 'picture' of what the wizard attempted to say: To the Rangers, that twin world will be really/really BIG. In fact, most lifeforms in the Milky Way will be Giants to him and his crew of 12.

(Why twelve? Why did Heart Center choose a 12-member crew, men and women, to travel to the new galaxy and organize there? Because there was a legendary band of escapees earmarked for symbiote hosts who were brought to their destruction over the South Pole. The Ranger crew honored those brave heroes).

Heart Center was not sad about the Master's death. Because it wasn't death; it was a *renewal.* He knew what was coming, the final words of Lin Wu:

"Here another.......................*joke...*"

The great man was dead.

Later...

Heart Center stood inside his high-tech quarters onboard the Lexington starship, a delta model with a Quantum Engine, everything needed for the assignment at hand. He was alone and stood in front of a large mirror. He was Captain and under his command was a very skilled and well-trained crew: Tomorrow's ARCHONS. His best friends that he would die for and he knew they would die for him. He observed his reverse image and made sure he'd never slip to the Dark Side whereby his 'anti' controlled his mind and body. He would always stay true to himself. That man was very, very good.

Soon the Lexington, a ship of destiny, would be off to another galaxy. The coordinates were set, locked and the unpiloted ship followed a pre-planned course through time and over space until it reached its proper destination, automatically.

Heart Center could enter his Sleep Chamber at any time. He decided now was as good a time as any - so he prepared for the Big Sleep. Once the cozy/comfy sheets and pillows were in place, the right buttons were pushed that activated the chamber. He pulled the clear top down [click] and plugged into the flow of nutrients that will sustain his life. He heard the clean air flow and adjusted the temperature. That was it.

"Goodnight," he said. To the Universe, he gave thanks. "Thank you."

The suspended animation was called "sleep," but it was not sleep in the normal sense. In minutes, Heart Center would succumb to the bio-chemicals in the airflow and the slowed-metabolism process would begin. *Will I dream?* he asked himself. He didn't know. *Maybe not, since it wasn't sleep. We'll see.*

His last conscious thoughts before the process took over concerned what exactly happened previously? He had to go over it again, just one more time...

How can I sort out the events I remember? How did Danos star systems become virtually clean and clear?

Then the true answer struck him from a credible source (his hearts): His dream was the answer. *Yes, my dream of long ago. It was like a cartoon! When Catwallender was a full, furry feline and showed me the Darkness that my presence there had caused...real evil, the weight of physical evil was sealed inside the dream. That was it. Material Evil went POOF when I woke! Gone, deleted, cancelled in a puff of smoke! Yes, the Dispenser People experienced darkness and fear in their colorful and beautiful dream world...but it was a Dream World and not a real one! Fantasy dispenser-heads suffered, not real people. So real people and aliens in the Danos Galaxy were cleaned of the dark presence...wow. That's what happened. Now I feel better. I understand...*

Oh, criminy drat, I just thought of Sebastian. It wasn't only darkness and fear that surrounded him, he was devoured! I know! Not real! Just a cartoon or CGI. But, I really liked the guy. That was too damn bad. Anyway, way...I feel woozy. Woozy...

17. The Last Dream

The Last Dream was a return to the colorful PEZ Planet and the wonderful people and things that inhabited the town of East McSweetport. Once more, there were blue-turquoise skies, fantastic creatures and the sweet smell of candy in the air. Not an atomic particle of Dark, anywhere. Way out ahead of the tall buildings and traffic on Cherry Boulevard and Lemon Lane, stood the Great Labyrinth and Ground Zero for activities. Millions of dispenser people and things lived there on floor after floor, high into the sky. Some did laundry and you'd view towels, sheets, shirts and pants that blew in the wind. Cook-outs and parties on terraces were common sights. A variety of games were played. Music often blasted out of windows. People and things in the apartments and compartments and condos loved it. Or, the creatures simply hung-out and had sparkling, intelligent conversations on balconies.

There was huge news in town: *The Ace will appear to everyone!* "Just imagine, the Ace!" News spread over every Media channel! Radios and TVs broadcast that the "Ace will fly into East McSweetport today" and "All should go to the Labyrinth and greet the famous Flying Ace."

That's exactly what creatures did on PEZ Planet. They went home and prepared for the party of a lifetime! If they did not live in the Maze, they knew people that did and joined them this grand day. They'd actually get a chance to glance at their hero in films and in real life. War hero. He single-handedly stopped the Great War by using his keen wits and brain-power and not weapons. The Ace was also a big hero to children. They loved to read of his clever capers in comic books and on the back of baseball cards. People and things were in place and very excited about seeing the celebrity zoom by! Their heads poked out and their eyes paid attention to the skies.

Up in the air...

A purple plane, 2-seater ["Spencer"] streaked through the stratosphere high over hills and valleys and lakes. The PEZ-shaped ship had two pilots at the controls: One was the Ace, who looked like a famous tennis player, and the other was his faithful friend and co-pilot, Sebastian. The crab was almost as famous as the Alpha Male. He played his role of 'second-banana' well (unlike Scottie Pippen), happy to be right by the side of his 'Captain,' the main man. Fans also enjoyed Sebastian's adventures in his own series of comic books, without Ace. They had made a few movies together and the cartoon world ate them up! The Flying Duo spoke to each other before they reached the main town...

Auto-pilot was clicked *off.* Now, Sebastian was at the controls. He thought it only fitting that he be the driver and taxi-in the big guy. Seb said, "This is much better than if I drove the royal carriage for the King and Queen..."

"Is it?" asked Ace. "You were going to be the royal driver, Seb?"

"Dude, that was in my dreams..."

"Seb, look over there," Ace directed the little guy.

"Ha! You know who that is?" His claw pointed at a special incoming jet plane.

Ace said, "We have a minute before we reach the Maze. I guess Starlord's Guardians thought we needed an escort?"

Sebastian responded, "I thought it was Rocket's Guardians? Hey! HEY!" the crab screamed at the Guardians, but really at his friend who flew the plane.

The jet streaked closer and glided very near the cockpit of Ace's PEZ-plane. They mutually waved a few miles over the surface.

Seb grabbed the radio, tuned to their frequency and yelled: "Hey, Rocket! Wanna race?!"

Rocket transmitted: *"I keep beating you every time! What's the sense in racing, I ask you?"*

Ace asked his partner, "He beats you?"

Seb clicked off the radio and replied: "Never. I told you, he's a funny guy." The crab clicked the radio back on. He told the Guardians: "We can take it from here, girls and boys..."

Ace added, "I think they're doing it just to *steal our thunder* and be on Social Media, like they're not already? Huh?"

"Hey. We heard that."

"Ha, ha. Later guys. Eat some dust." Sebastian hit turbo and left the Guardians nearly at a standstill.

The famous Flying Duo approached the Labyrinth and struck the breaks, which slowed the plane down considerably. They cruised at a comfortable speed as the plane maneuvered over the 8-laned highway entrance and then chose a particular avenue and flew over it. Ace and Sebastian flew between floor after floor of the complex Maze that held millions of dwellings on high walls. People and things went crazy! Such adoring fans! They cheered, waved, partied, shot confetti cannons, lit fireworks that streamed high into the sky and *exploded!* The PEZ people and things danced and played music and more music. It was the greatest. Everyone was happy!

Pez 4 Ever

Ace and Sebastian spent an hour in flight and zipped through corridor after corridor, passageway after passageway, and occasionally stopped at a lucky balcony and signed autographs and had photos taken. After all, Social Media was important, right?

They spent much more time than was planned and they gave more to the people and things than anyone had ever expected. Ace took control of Spencer, the flying tablet, and landed it on an empty part of the Maze's yellow roof. He wanted to be alone with Sebastian after all the super excitement and boosts to the ego. He wanted to relax now. He calmed down, dialed it back and had a sincere and serious moment with the crab. Ace wondered:

"What if this beauty and perfection are only dreams, Sebastian?"

The red-orange, little fellow quickly replied: "Does it really matter if it's a dream or not, pal? We're here. We're real. We're happy...and it's a wonderful world. Right?"

Ace was about to cry, after everything that's happened. He agreed with his best friend and said, "Right." He extended his hand. "Shake."

Seb lifted his claw and they shook hands. They held it for a while.

Ace told his buddy the truth: "I wouldn't have made it this far if not for you."

Tears streamed down Sebastian's face.

Ace felt it too.

[Some dreams do not change into nightmares].

The End

**Due to a change in reality (editing),
the Queen's 'Universal Acceleratron'
was never utilized ~ *thank goodness.***

Books written by TS Caladan (DH Jetson):

The Continuum

Son of Zog

The Cydonian War

Science-Faction [Vol. 1 & 2] short stories

ANAGRAMACRON

inspiration

2099, Transia~

The New Men and the New World

Beyond Barronsland

Mandela Effect

Best of TS Caladan

Mandela Effect II

Collected Comedy of TS Caladan

TS Caladan's Comedy II

Pez Wars

The PEZ-Effect

Ceana

PEZ 4 Ever

TS Caladan

Doug was born the only son of Rose and Steve Yurchey in Bridgeville, PA. in 1951. A loner, he drew pictures and dreamed of big/bright fantasy-worlds that were inside the comic book adventures he cherished. Movies, TV, thrilled the young man, especially sci-fi and anything that had to do with aliens and life on other planets. He grew up interested in sports and earned a half-scholarship in tennis to Edinboro. After college, his interests turned to astronomy and various mysteries.

An unexpected event occurred: In 1973, he fell in love with a psychic who channeled. A 4-year marriage and a 'virtual Close Encounter' later, the young man was motivated to discover the truth in everything<. Odd occurrences happened during a strange marriage where spoons and keys bent with the powers of the mind. They met mentalist Uri Geller at this time. Wife Katrina did similar telepathic feats and their closest friends witnessed extraordinary things. In 1977, the marriage ended.

Doug moved to LA in 1982. He worked on the Simpsons Show in 1990-1991 as a background artist. He became a prolific writer with many online articles, radio interviews and YouTubes of his work on Atlantis, Nikola Tesla and the World Grid. His dream came true and he was published by TWB Press in 2015. Now *TS Caladan,* the author's interests are Modern Mysteries and conspiracies or secrets behind Hollywood and the Illuminati. Then he discovered the Mandela Effect, which *changed everything~.* Tray Caladan is a mystery himself. He has spent more than 50 years of pure, honest, scientific research and today uses artwork and wild, sci-fi stories to deliver his conclusions...*and no one believes him.*

Contact information for Tray Samuel Caladan:

tscaladan@gmail.com

Questions and comments are very welcome. Readers will receive quick replies. Thank you very much.

~tsc

Enjoy more short stories and novels by
many talented authors at

https://www.twbpress.com

Science Fiction, Supernatural, Horror, Thrillers, Romance,
and more